a collector of affections

Tales from a Woman's Heart

JUDITH GLYNN

Always maximize the journey

Judith Glynn

Published by Fox Point Press
foxpointpress.com

Cover and book design by Infinitum Limited

ISBN 978-0-9834595-0-7

Please visit the website:
judithglynn.com

This book is dedicated to the late John M. Roderick, a gifted teacher, and one who guided my first attempts to write a story. Thank you, John, for your patience, softness, skill and friendship.

Acknowledgements

An author takes an inner journey when turning blank pages into a book, but others also contribute to the work, often unknowingly.

I thank my children. Without the freedom and unconditional love they give me, I'd be diminished. I extend my deepest gratitude to Peggy Smith and Peggie Anderson for their early support. Pilar Vico's unending friendship and prods kept this story alive. Other great ladies who spurred me on are Linda Ayares, Joan Bankemper and Diane J. Findlay. And to Basil Northam, a man without equal, for his insight, humor and deep friendship.

A writer stumbles without colleagues. Ron Stodghill said to take along a toolbox filled with dialogue, description, exposition and characterization when I wrote. Terri Valentine's editing skills shaped the manuscript. Jeannie Friedman's line edits resembled red ants crossing the pages.

Finally, a writer needs inspiration. For that, I thank the Universe.

CHAPTER ONE

IT WASN'T THAT UNUSUAL FOR LEAH LYNCH to return her seatmate's handshake. She'd done it before with other polite strangers, especially on long flights. The serendipity of the gesture often led to an interesting conversation. This time the plane would depart from New York, journey through darkened skies across the Atlantic and land in Madrid the following morning.

"Hi, I'm Miguel Santiago," her seatmate said and extended his hand. Until then, she'd paid little attention to him. "Great night to fly, isn't it?"

"Perfect night. Nice to meet you. I'm Leah Lynch," she said returning his firm handshake. An unsettling vibe rocked her clear to her toes when their eyes met. But she didn't outwardly react to his touch or the intensity she'd experienced. She simply smiled back, slid her hand away from his and went back to arranging a few items in her seat pocket.

"First trip to Spain?" he asked and raised his seat to the upright position as the flight attendants banged overhead bins shut.

"No, I've taken this journey many times," she said, startled at the sexual sparks that simply radiated from him.

Miguel's olive-skinned face with its ear-to-ear smile was pleasing to the eye. A few gray strands speckled his thick brown hair combed straight back with soft curls barely touching the top of his starched pinstriped shirt. Penetrating and spirited dark brown eyes complemented his wildly handsome look. A professional aura surrounded him. Successful people had that same unmistakable trait. She guessed his age to be mid-fifties, close to hers. His voice was a smoky baritone, the type heard in compelling commercials. Any receptive woman would love a sexy phone call from him at two in the morning asking if she'd like a visitor for the rest of the night.

"Please raise your seat," the attendant said to Leah, returning her to the reality of the moment.

Complying, she then readied herself for the long flight by removing her shoes and slipping on flimsy, brown airline socks. No stranger to flying or to visiting Spain, she wrote travel articles and popular romance novels that took place in the country. Years ago she'd lived in Madrid and returned often. The ancient stone buildings, the intense sunlight, the purity of the moonlight and the country's sensual underbelly soothed and excited her soul. But regardless of the visit's purpose, romance was the one constant pleasure. Whether she simply flirted with men, made love or enjoyed looking at them, she and Spain understood one another. Spain was her Mecca.

But this three-week trip to Madrid produced anxiety she couldn't shake or explain. When the town car arrived to drive her to the airport, she was waiting outside her apartment building. For most pick-ups – she'd stopped taking taxis and preferred the luxury of a town car – she kept the driver waiting. This time, he jumped out of the car when he saw her, adjusted her two suitcases in the trunk and opened the door for her to slide across the leather back seat.

"Just confirming, madam. Newark Airport, international departures?" he asked over his shoulder before pulling into traffic.

"That's right," she said and checked her travel documents one last time.

~ ♡ ~

A sense of adventure always swept over Leah when she flew. This night was no exception as the engines roared with increased velocity, and the passengers grew silent. As the plane taxied down the runway, she glanced out the oval window at the jagged skyline backlit by a crimson sunset. New York had been her home for many years. But she needed the solitude about to engulf her in Spain, especially since she spoke limited Spanish, to work through her mental agenda and reach a deeper level of self-evaluation.

The decades of freedom after her divorce had produced plenty of giggles, terrific sex — even a brief engagement — but that lifestyle was now stale. Although she vowed never to remarry, a committed companion-lover was a more realistic goal as she moved along in middle age. "Change your thoughts to change your life." This was her new motto.

Then there was her daughter Dana's wedding day. Leah dreaded the upcoming event. It meant a return to her Rhode Island hometown. Her divorce from Jim, Dana's father, was in their healed past and he'd remarried. Leah, however, would attend the wedding alone. Many Rhode Islanders would question her success and worldly views without a man on her arm.

The last tug at her conscience about the trip to Spain – actually, it was the first but she couldn't admit it – was seeing Javier Lorca after a long hiatus. They had shared a lustful affair when she lived in Madrid right after her divorce, and they stayed in touch over the years. When he learned about her upcoming trip to Madrid, he asked if she'd spend the night with him in Salamanca. The beautiful medieval city was a three-hour drive northwest of Madrid.

"I'll get two rooms. You decide where to sleep. We have lots to discuss after all these years. I want you to know you're still in my heart," he said.

"It's different for us now, isn't it?" she said and paused. "Enough for me to meet you in Salamanca."

Once the plane was aloft, the flight attendant's refreshment cart rattled down the aisle. Leah avoided alcohol on overnight flights after years of groggy landings. A sleeping pill was in her purse. She'd take it and hope for a few hours' sleep before the Madrid arrival. The cabin crew knew not to disturb her for dinner.

"Would you like a drink?" seatmate Miguel asked Leah.

"Sure, why not? I'll have a red wine."

"And I'll have Dewar's on the rocks," he said, and paid for both drinks.

"Thank you for the treat."

"My pleasure. To a safe trip," he toasted as they clicked plastic glasses.

"Absolutely to a safe trip." She noticed he wasn't wearing a wedding ring.

"So what about you? Is this your first trip to Spain?" Leah asked and turned in her seat to look at him. She felt slightly obligated to begin a conversation because of his generosity.

There was also a celebratory ambiance starting to take shape.

"Second trip. Last year I completed the Camino de Santiago pilgrim's trail. It took me three weeks. I walked half of the arduous route and bicycled the rest." His overland journey began in Leon, a northern province in Spain, and ended in Santiago de Compostela, a city located in Galicia, not far from the Atlantic.

"You must be a spiritual man," Leah surmised, knowing the solitary pilgrimage required a special stamina to reach the cathedral and St. James' tomb. When completed, Miguel joined a select group acknowledged for over one thousand years.

"I'm not devout. I did it to test my physical endurance and because I love to travel in Spain. Plus, the cathedral carries part of my last name, which I find amusing."

Perhaps it was the closeness of their seats that kept them talking after take-off and where Leah learned Miguel was a native-born Spaniard who'd immigrated to Virginia as a boy with his family. But America never settled in his heart. He balanced his unrest as an adult with frequent trips to Mediterranean countries. The family-owned Santiago Bros. Jewelry Company was his to run when he returned from Spain, yet he expressed little passion for the new position. Had his family not dictated his career, Miguel would have pursued one in the arts. He owned a valuable collection of modern art and scoured exhibits for emerging painters. His musical tastes included opera, jazz and country. He read voraciously, mostly classics or avant-garde literature, disliked sports and only watched independent films.

"Have you ever been married?" Leah asked.

"Once. It was brief and decades ago. No children either. I'm not sure I know how to choose the right woman." Now middle-aged and after a succession of girlfriends, he lived with Susan Ingram, a divorced mother of three grown children who were on their own. "Last night while I packed she asked if we'd be married soon," he said.

"That's a fair question. You live together. Will you marry her?"

"I said I wasn't ready," he answered sharply. "Strange, isn't it? This trip doesn't include her, and we just moved in together."

"I'm surprised. Don't you travel with her?"

"Of course we take trips but I don't like the long ones where it's 24/7 togetherness. I like my solitude. I've never lasted more than four years with any woman. No matter how much she loves me, it's never enough," he sighed. "I wish I could find the right woman. Susan is a wonderful person, but I'm not sure she's it."

"You don't love yourself enough," Leah said, somewhat startled by her quick and judgmental observation of his love life. "You have to begin from within before you can love someone else unconditionally." His perplexed expression made her add that maybe Susan was right for him. "Give it time," she said.

"We'll see," was his too-quick reply.

Miguel and Leah didn't watch the movie when the tiny screens lowered into the cabin. Instead, they revealed more about themselves with an uncommon openness for new seatmates. It enlightened Leah to learn how others lived their lives. The depth of Miguel's truthfulness became evident as their conversation deepened.

"So what about you?" he asked glancing at her with a wry smile. "What's your story? What will you do in Spain?"

Something compelled her to open up about herself. He made her feel so free. "I've been divorced for years. My children are grown. I'm a freelance travel writer and novelist. I live in New York," she said with an air of confidence. "I also have a former self when I lived a dismal life in tiny Rhode Island as a simple homemaker and mother. That was before I moved to New York," she added. It never crossed her mind that Miguel couldn't handle that detail.

What she omitted was being any woman or every woman struggling to find the courage to divorce her husband. She was a beaten-down and broke woman gasping to breathe renewed life into her troubled soul. Once she won those battles, both internal and external, she changed forever. She took bold and unheard of risks to survive on her own and help her live life as she saw fit. She would never again blindly follow a path chosen for her by others. She left Rhode Island and relinquished the care of her teenage children to her ex-husband.

With her divorce came financial freedom. Her career as a writer took off. But she imagined the ultimate freedom would be finding a true and unconditional love with the right man. Until she found him or he found her, she'd be a collector of affections. She'd love herself unconditionally and take chances with her heart. She didn't tell Miguel that philosophy.

"I'm an f.o.s.," she said hoping to deflect further in-depth personal questions.

"What's that?"

"Friend of Spain. I love the country. I discover more about myself with each visit. Don't get me wrong though. I couldn't accomplish a physical journey like yours on the Camino but I do make equally thrilling choices. That's why I return often. Spain is a gorgeous place to get lost in."

"Hmmmm. You sound like an interesting woman. You'll have to tell me more about yourself and those adventures. Do you have a boyfriend?" he asked sheepishly.

"Not really. I'm a risk taker, even in love," she said. "It's a different approach than most women take. I'll opt for bliss over boredom any day. I'm going to meet someone at a Salamanca hotel after we land tomorrow. Separate rooms, by the way. We were lovers a long time ago when I lived in Madrid. We were both newly divorced. When I returned to the States, he remarried his ex-wife and moved back in with their four children. But he'd call me faithfully on my birthday. It kept our friendship alive through the years. He's not a cad. He's a nice guy. Just words between good friends."

"He obviously loved you; otherwise, he wouldn't call. Loving two women at the same time isn't that hard. We men fantasize about a woman like you. But here comes the reality after so many years. What's going to happen in Salamanca?"

"I should have mentioned earlier that his wife died in a car crash with two of their children. We'll see what happens," was all she volunteered.

She didn't tell him about the ultimatum she planned to spring on Javier. The time had come for a serious commitment. She also wanted to take him to her daughter's wedding. How could she have divulged so many intimate details to this seatmate named Miguel? But it didn't really matter since they'd land and go their separate ways.

"Interesting tale, Leah. Good luck renewing whatever you had, but a dead wife is still in his picture. And that hotel in Salamanca you mentioned? I have a reservation there, too, but a week later."

"Really? It's a former convent. Don't tell them you're not devout. You'll be asked to publicly recite the rosary before they let you in."

When the film ended, the screens returned to their ceiling slots. The cabin lights dimmed and softened the plane's ambiance. Passengers adjusted their bodies into cramped seats, ripped open plastic blanket bags, tucked tiny pillows behind their necks or folded them against a window. Some chose to read by a narrow beam of light streaming from overhead. Miguel and Leah covered their bodies with small blankets but didn't close their eyes. They spoke in softer tones so as not to disturb nearby passengers.

"Why did you leave Rhode Island and move to New York? Forgive me for prying but that was a ballsy mid-life change for a divorced woman with kids," he said.

"My divorce was amicable. We agreed to disagree about our marriage. It took years of arguments to reach a point where the split benefited both of us. I wanted marriage, children, a large amount of freedom and the opportunity to pursue my newfound writing career. My husband wanted me home as a married woman with children and no career. We never agreed on how to live our married lives but could move forward without one another. Actually, his parenting skills at the time were better. I always wanted to live in New York. That's where the publishing world is. Our teenage children were fine with the divorce and my moving away," she said softly as the intimacy of her new friendship with Miguel grew. She instinctively began to trust him. He understood her soul. He wouldn't judge her harshly.

"When I arrived in New York, I had no home, no furniture, not even a spoon. I only had enough money to survive and myself to count on. My first novel flopped so I licked my wounds, wrote a second and succeeded with many bestsellers."

"Were you still involved with your children? Did you see

them often?"

"Of course I was involved and saw them a lot. In fact, my daughter lives in New York now. My son lives in California. I didn't miss a beat as their mother. My husband did a wonderful job as Mr. Mom. We were trailblazers with that lifestyle and didn't know it."

"You're refreshingly revealing and a remarkable woman."

"Thanks. And one more thing I resolved. I'd be my own best friend. Try it. It works. I'm now a happy, well-adjusted, self-assured woman and thankful to be so. My mind and heart are finally in sync," she said.

Yet something was missing. Her two children were once her focus, but they were now grown, which should have simplified her decision about who she'd become next. But she still floundered. Leah didn't mention Dana's wedding to Miguel. It was too much information to reveal. She was also looking for tenderness in her life. She did tell him that. When he grew silent with her comment, she didn't elaborate. Instead, her mind drifted to the recent phone conversation she had with Rocío, a *madrileña* friend now in her late sixties.

Their friendship began when Leah lived in Madrid years ago. Rocío loved practicing her fluent English with Leah, which didn't help Leah improve her bumbling Spanish. They kept in contact when Rocío located to New York with her husband. She began a career importing Spanish antiques. She also began an affair with a Spaniard from Barcelona. When discovered, it destroyed her marriage and forced her back to Spain, practically penniless. With her feet firmly planted in the antique business, she managed to resurrect herself as a financially secure woman, sending rare Spanish antiquities to the best galleries in the States. She married a second time only to see it fail in eighteen months, souring her on men and falling in love again.

"Don't you miss tenderness in your life?" Leah had asked her friend.

"Sometimes, but I have cats to fill that need."

"Oh, come on. Level with me. Don't you want a man in your life again? He could make you happier."

"If we are always happy, we are stupid. We should struggle with something. That's how we get inspiration from life," Rocío said. Spaniards often used *we* to lump others into their philosophy. "As for being in love, that's a sickness. Why haven't you figured that out yet?"

"Because I'm a hopeless romantic, that's why. You used to be one, too, Rocío. Get that feeling back. It's important to our well-being."

"You're a silly woman, Leah. Forget romance now. You're too old."

"No I'm not. Hope springs eternal with me. But let's discuss this tenderness subject when I arrive in Madrid. See you soon."

At one point in the flight when Miguel returned to his seat after a body-stretching stroll in the aisle, he put his arm around Leah's shoulder and leaned into her.

"You fall in love too fast," she said, giggling a little self-consciously at his boyish and physical gesture. Even though he was handsome, savvy, a charmer, risqué, well dressed, funny and a terrific conversationalist, she regretted telling him about her tenderness yearnings. Putting his arm around her was daring for a seatmate to do, but it felt good. She wasn't about to ask for a seat change so late in the flight. Miguel wasn't a predator; they were both simply in happy moods. Their comradery was building as the flight continued. She assumed her conservative and stylish look, green eyes and black hair appealed to him.

She was only mildly concerned about the few extra pounds she'd gained with age. Her softer and lower body type was a metaphor for her approach to life. She was now softer to be around and her expectations not as high as they'd been when she was younger.

In the darkened cabin, Leah daydreamed about the purity of her conversation with Miguel. It deserved the purest of compliments. If she had brushed her soft lips over his, which was their personal and adult truth at that moment, he'd have accepted her gift without question. He had such nice, full, welcoming lips. But that was the scene she wrote in her head, not reality.

"Hi again," he whispered and breathed a conciliatory exhale after a long silence. He then lowered his questioning eyes and sighed.

"Who knew we'd enjoy this flight so immensely, but we need to doze off," she said and closed her eyes just before his lips moved in a blow-away kiss. It felt so natural to relax in her seat, cross her left leg over her right and allow her shoulder to touch his. They'd boarded as strangers but quickly became more than casual traveling companions. It was all so odd to feel such a strong attraction for him so fast, and on a plane. What was happening? Whatever it was, it created a great flight. She'd use the scene in one of her novels.

When dawn's light seeped in throughout the cabin, the overhead screens lowered again to show a tiny plane on an animated path nearing southern Europe. Miguel and Leah had traveled in a cocoon-like airplane row headed toward their Promised Lands. Hers was Spain where she experienced her heart and emotions at their deepest level. His was the Mediterranean soil where his soul flourishes anew, especially since his European roots had been ripped out of him when he moved to Virginia as a child.

With little time left in the flight, Miguel tucked a pillow behind his neck and closed his eyes. Leah did the same and listened to his deep breathing while he napped, but his presence and allure led her to uncross her legs and move her right knee to rest against his.

"Are you awake?" Miguel whispered, as the plane began its descent over Spain. We're almost there," he said and gently leaned against her in order to open the window shade.

She liked his warm body next to hers. When the flight attendants walked through the aisles handing out immigration forms, she and Miguel flipped their trays down to complete theirs with a shared pen. Below, Spain's ochre-colored landscape with its wavy groves of olive trees grew closer with the descent.

As the plane taxied to the gate, Miguel removed his thick book from his seat pocket. A Metropolitan Museum of Art bookmark, the colorful costumed knight in armor, poked out from the pages. Leah's book held a Met bookmark but it was the Statue of Liberty. He then adjusted the time on his Rolex six hours ahead to coincide with Spain's time zone. Next, he smoothed both hands over his thighs and paused to remove a speck of link from his pressed jeans. She found it attractive that his nails were clipped short with no frayed cuticles.

They were inseparable walking through the terminal and as they waited at the luggage carousel.

"Your hotel is close to my apartment," she told him. "Let's share a cab into Madrid. You speak Spanish better than I do and my street is hard to find. I'm exhausted. Congratulations, Miguel, you're quite the conservationist to keep me awake for the entire flight."

"It wasn't just me. You're quite the captivator to keep me talking to you."

As the cab pulled curbside, she invited him up to her temporary home. He rolled her large suitcase across the lobby's marble floor and waited as she guided her computer bag into the brass birdcage elevator. When he closed the outer door, a metallic clank echoed in the hallway as the latch caught. Miguel then pushed the two inner wooden doors shut and pressed the button for the fifth and top floor.

"How's this for closeness? What happens if we get stuck?" he joked as he, Leah and her luggage were crammed into the tiny elevator inching its way upward.

Her temporary Madrid home had four rooms that ran along a hallway filled with contemporary art. Miguel took in each piece. Both the living room and bedroom doors led to separate patios, each with terra-cotta floor tiles and potted plants hearty enough to withstand the blazing Spanish sunshine.

After Leah yawned repeatedly, she told Miguel she needed to nap in order to meet Javier in Salamanca later that day. "Here's my Spain cell phone number," she said and scribbled nine numbers on the back of her business card as he stood at the door. "Perhaps we can meet up when I return to Madrid tomorrow. You're still here, right?" She'd traveled alone for years and knew the importance of meeting someone at the end of a sightseeing day. Offering her friendship was easy. She liked his company. He was easy on the eye and very easy on the ear.

"I'll be in Madrid for several days before I travel throughout Castilla y Leon and Castilla-LaMancha. I'd hate to think I'd never see you again. Imagine changing my seat as a favor and meeting you. I won't lose this number," he said and put her card in his shirt pocket. He then put his hands on her shoulders.

"We're in Spain now. A kiss on each cheek is appropriate. Two kisses are twice as nice," he said and almost put one on her mouth as he went from one side of her face to the other to kiss her good-bye.

"That was a wonderful plane ride. I look forward to seeing you again," she said, hoping Miguel didn't sense how flustered she became with him so close.

CHAPTER TWO

AFTER MIGUEL LEFT, LEAH WALKED over to a large bedroom window and yanked on a cloth tape to lower the outside roller shade. She then drew the drapes, showered and slid naked under the soft bed covers for a long nap.

She spoke with Javier by phone to confirm their Salamanca rendezvous that evening. Her enthusiasm didn't match his. She blamed it on jet lag, a sleepless flight and the aftermath of two glasses of wine. What she didn't include in her list was the seven-hour, non-stop conversation with Miguel Santiago as they flew from one continent to another. She imagined him napping and naked in his hotel bed before venturing out into Madrid later that day. Was he thinking about her, too?

Leah had met Javier in Madrid shortly after her divorce when she was there for a work assignment. Their happenstance side-by-side hotel check-in led to a friendly discussion that led to dinner that led to bed weeks later. He was a wonderfully kind, peaceful and divorced Spaniard. They traveled through Europe and vacationed at countryside villas in Spain. She enjoyed his credit card to shop in Paris. For the opera in Rome, there were box seats. They also sunbathed nude on deserted beaches in Andalusia. Javier introduced her to a higher level of lovemaking and an intimacy she'd look for in future lovers.

"Please don't leave me," he'd say often. "I don't know what I'll do without you in Spain. I love you deeply."

But when her assignment ended, she wanted to go home, ever grateful to Javier and Spain for healing her newly divorced soul. If he'd asked her to marry him, she would have stayed. But he didn't. She didn't want a long-distance affair. Instead, she became her own best friend, something new, which emboldened her to break the news to Javier.

"I don't know how to say this so I'll blurt it out. I'm leaving for New York to start a new life in a few days. We'll stay in touch."

"Would you have left and not told me?"

She felt the deep groan he sighed but remained silent. He was devastated. She wasn't.

"Don't ever get married, Leah. You don't need it. You have everything, and most of all, you have freedom," were his parting words.

In the beginning of their separation, Javier called Leah weekly, asking her to return to Madrid or to meet him anywhere she wanted. She'd refuse. Her New York life had taken off in many directions and not one pointed toward Spain. When she agreed to meet him in Salamanca after his wife died, he fixated on Leah as a budding divorcee, crazy in love with him and their former life in Madrid. He kept her enshrined in a time-warped past.

"I'm different now," she told him.

"But not to me," he whispered into the phone.

Leah didn't force a new dialogue because she, too, had time-warped their affair. She'd slept with and loved other men after him. She didn't consider Javier a potential partner until he became a widower. Like Rhode Island, he was also part of *her former self.* But she didn't want a marriage anymore; when she agreed to their liaison, she merely wanted a tender companion.

Leah awoke from her nap and thought about Miguel. He was so much fun. What was he doing in Madrid at that precise moment? Was he thinking about her?

"What's with these Miguel thoughts?" she scolded herself in the bathroom mirror as she smoothed a buff-colored foundation under her eyes and over her face. She turned her thoughts to Javier. Would he think she'd aged? Would he notice the extra pounds she'd gained? Was he looking in his mirror, too?

The bus she boarded at Madrid's AutoRes station would take several hours to reach Salamanca. The young woman seated beside her flipped open a fluorescent-green cell phone and began a text message. Her khaki-colored skirt was hiked above her knees, showing bronzed legs accented with cloth *espadrilles* laced around shapely ankles. A magazine's headline on her lap promised to reveal five new ways to please a man in bed. Leah wondered what she could learn from that article. To understand lovemaking meant to experience its power; it was knowledge that grew within a woman if she submitted. She was a far better lover in her womanhood.

Outside the bus windows, hundreds of black, shiny bulls grazed on farmland or stood motionless under the stone pine trees. Later on, long stretches of vibrant yellow sunflowers faced the sun in perfect alignment. Far into the distance, the ever-present olive trees grew haphazardly from gnarled trunks anchored in parched ochre soil. It looked like a giant comb had drawn deep grooves through the land.

Leah and Salamanca were not strangers. She discovered

the ancient city when she first arrived in Spain to write travel articles. The Castilla-Leon province published Spain's first grammar book in 1492. Visitors to the medieval city headed to the eighteenth-century Plaza Mayor to experience the wondrous Gothic architecture. Four stone stories enclosed the open-square lined with balconies and full-length, weathered, wooden shutters. Below its arches, small shops, restaurants and outdoor cafes with metal tables and chairs kept the square densely populated. Main squares were Spain's outdoor living rooms where people stroll, strut, gossip, browse, flirt, shop, parade or watch the rest of the world go by. According to most Spaniards, Salamanca has the country's finest plaza.

She loved sitting at one of the outdoor restaurants watching the mass invasion of Spaniards as they approached the square from all sides. The women were dressed to the nines in tweeds, silks and the best of European fashion. Hair was sprayed in place and gold jewelry glittered. Their men were held tightly by the arm and invariably wore belted trench coats. Old parents and friends were arm-in-arm.

There was a lot of posturing. Children were pushed in carriages or held up to be tickled and have their cheeks squeezed or kissed. Long, navy-blue Melton coats with gold buttons were common. Little girls had tiny, gold earrings pierced into their lobes. Young children were quieted with pacifiers worn like a necklace. That fetish, in those days, had won national acceptance. There didn't seem to be a natural thumb sucker left in the country.

Within fifteen minutes, the plaza was jammed. A human beehive. If viewed from above, the mass had one common direction: round and round. Cafes and restaurants did a brisk business. There were no con men selling wind-up toys, no balloons, no beggars, just talkers and strollers. Leah was enthralled.

Almost by instinct with the striking of two on the big clock over the Town Hall, the crowd thinned, slowly retracing its steps back down the narrow side streets. They took with them their chatter and the essence of Spanish life – the need to flaunt civic, social and family obligations with great public display.

Spain and Salamanca were less formal in dress and rituals when Leah returned to rendezvous with Javier. The city's familiar honey-colored buildings appeared as the bus crossed over the River Tormes Bridge and pulled into the station. She waited for the other passengers to disembark, using the time to smear on a touch of lipstick and fluff her hair. She slung her travel bag over one shoulder and took the escalator to the terminal's main floor. A tourist kiosk provided walking directions to the restaurant Javier had suggested. He thought it would be easier – *softer* was the word he chose – for their reunion to take place in public rather than at the hotel.

Her heart pounded as she strolled to the restaurant while taking in the beauty of Salamanca's long passageways bordered by shops and ancient buildings. Leah was disgusted with herself for feeling so anxious about the upcoming meeting. So much time had passed, hard-earned time where she gained a world of sophistication and skills to deal with anxiety. So what was going on? Please, dear heart, don't revisit images of our intense affair. What she needed was a reality jolt: see Javier, reminisce, smile a lot and stop this foolishness. They weren't lovers any more but maybe he was a potential lifetime companion.

She passed a former seventeenth-century convent. The building had become a language school where scantily clad and giggling students spilled onto the cobblestoned street. Was that a sacrilege? In the distance, just past the terra-cotta tile roofs, a stork's nest draped over a church spire. If the wind blew in her direction, she heard the storks' clucking. The huge bells of the Catedral de Salamanca chimed deeply and resonantly throughout the city; they rang inside of her as well and produced a calm to allay her fears.

"Psssst," was the only sound she made when Javier entered the restaurant. He turned and froze in place when he recognized her. His appearance had changed although she'd forgotten his exact looks, having destroyed all photos of him. His hair was grayer. He was heavier. His stomach protruded more than she remembered. Would she have known him had he passed her on the street? Probably not. But like the toy clown popping out of the jack-in-the-box, Leah jumped up to hug him.

"You look the same," he said.

"Impossible."

A wide smile covered her face. What he didn't see was the gush of hot emotion racing through her body. The euphoria bubbled up inside her along with fear of the unknown. She cupped Javier's face in her hands. "I'm so happy to see you."

"Happy to see you, too. You have the most brilliant eyes. How did they stay that way through the years?"

"The light hasn't gone out. I'm happy with my life. So many people are finished by our age. I'm not. Hope springs eternal."

"I'm free now, Leah," he blurted out during dinner. He felt guilty saying the word despite his wife's death being a year old. "But I don't know what to do with this freedom." His insecurities about being a single father of two teenagers poured out of him with his clenched hands cupped on the table and his fingers forming a stiff semi-circle. His wife had handled the family and home issues. He now employed a housekeeper but she couldn't fill the missing emotional needs.

"How do you see your future as a man and not only a father?" Leah asked, hoping to be included in his dream.

Javier paused and signaled for the waiter to bring a glass of *anise.* He sipped the licorice-tasting drink. His smile indicated he liked what his mind's eye had created. "The ideal life should be lived communal-style with many people living in the same house. If someone needs love, they should make love with any person. Love is what's important in life. Tenderness, too, should be in the community."

"I can only relate to the tenderness part," she said trying to hide her disappointment. *Oh my God. He wants a communal life. Here he goes leaving me again. This time it's not to return to his ex-wife, but to many other women.*

To walk off the long lunch, they strolled around Salamanca's back streets holding hands. Spaniards stretch the hours of the day like gum. Javier was no exception. Leah often walked a few paces behind him. She was fairy-tale Hansel trailing breadcrumbs to find the way back to her center.

"So many years have passed. It's amazing to have you beside me in the flesh," were the only words she spoke when he stopped to hug her.

"We're older and better now. Come on, Leah. Let's try again. We're both single, know each other well, and I love you. We're still passionate lovers. I can feel it. Come to my room with me," he said sweetly.

"I need to clear my head with more walking, but alone. I'll keep my room in case we're only friends and not the lovers you remember."

This was her moment of deep truth. Hopping into bed with Javier again might resurrect their affair. But would it convince

22

him to start a committed and long-lasting relationship with her? That's what her heart and soul wanted. Or was their affair-based relationship so engrained in their psyches that neither could change its essence. Any thought of another marriage frightened her. She'd seen friends divorce and jump into a new marital bed out of desperation, only to find it wasn't any better. Leah couldn't face a similar disappointment. She adored her single life. But was her collector-of-affections lifestyle a foolish and destructive illusion? Everyone needed someone to love. But was it possible to have a steady companion without marriage? What would happen to her freedom?

She concluded Javier couldn't be a casual lover. She wanted more. She wanted them to be a public couple in Spain and in New York. She wanted his family to recognize her as the woman he'd chosen to love after his wife's death. The time had come to show it. She didn't like the *communal life* he talked about at dinner. Or was that a fantasy of playful words men say when talking about making love as they pleased?

Leah returned to the hotel and walked down the long corridor to Javier's room still questioning her decision to sleep with him again. Somehow, she was honor-bound because of his vigil over the years. She had a strange, self-imposed code for a lover with deep meaning, which was now a gray-haired and heavier Javier. He knew her better than she knew herself, however. The door was slightly ajar, a gesture from the past when he expected her arrival.

"Hi, sweetie," he said and jumped up from his chair when she knocked softly and pushed the door open. He stood up so fast, the hunting magazine on his lap flopped onto the floor. "I've been waiting for you for years," he said and hugged Leah so tightly that she gasped.

"Wow. That's some greeting," she blurted as he held her tighter.

The touch of his lips after so many years felt odd. That surprised her. Javier moaned softly as he kissed her harder and longer. Words poured out of him about their past lovemaking. Her touches. Her kisses. Her eyes. Her scent. He whispered a rolling list of superlatives into her ear. A heavy fog lifted from her cautious heart as Javier's hands discovered her again. She wanted to be younger, thinner, fuller on top and wetter on the bottom like she was when he first made love to her.

"I love you so much, so much," he said and stroked her face before he embraced her again, this time with softer and sweeter kisses. "There's no one like you, Leah," he said and gently slipped his hand inside her blouse to unfasten her bra.

Those embraces, his tender words and warm smile, gestures she knew so well, put a hold on her earlier decision. Waiting until the morning to discuss a long-term relationship wouldn't be so bad. Why sabotage a delicious night of lovemaking?

~ ♡ ~

"Rub my back, please. I love your touch," he said after their lovemaking subsided and he lay on his stomach. One hand was under his pillow, the other at his side. When she began the ritual, her sleepy eyes wandered about the room scented with lust. They stopped at the mirrored closet that reflected the curve of her nude body pressed against his. In the closet, Javier's Loden green wool coat hung beside her Cole Haan black bouclé jacket – temporary items placed there by a temporary hotel room couple.

Her soft fingertips swirled over his body until they found his hand where she traced his fingers, going up and down each one. She looked out the tiny window where an ancient bell tower stood in the courtyard reflecting moonbeams. A part of her soul was home. The hypnotic rhythm of Javier's breathing and the blanket of stars her mind created to warm the two of them, took her thoughts to another place.

She drifted away from the power of his body to soar over the bell tower, across Spain and the Atlantic until she glided to a soft landing in Rhode Island. She remembered herself there as a young woman, one who never dreamed beyond the state's borders. What to make for dinner, how to care for her children and how to build a married life consumed her daily thoughts. She didn't know anyone there with a passport. She didn't know anyone who lived in Europe. There wasn't the slightest interest to travel outside her New England roots. The seasonal landscapes offered foot-long icicles and majestic elms shedding colorful leaves and lobster pots yanked from Narragansett Bay.

Nothing about her early marriage suggested it would implode and that she'd live in Spain where glistening Spanish bulls with razor-sharp horns grazed alongside country roads. Nor was it clear when she applied for a passport, after her divorce, that the document would fill with foreign entry stamps before it expired. And there certainly wasn't any inkling when she walked down the aisle as a young, dewy-eyed bride that she'd pull up the bed covers years later lying next to a man who wasn't her husband. In fact, absolutely nothing about her early days as a wife and young mother would foreshadow the rich life she'd lead once she took control of it and moved away.

Just before she dozed off, Leah looked at the nearby mahogany desk. A long leather case rested on top. It held Javier's hunting rifle. After they'd part in the morning, he'd join his wealthy friends for a boar hunt. She wanted to go with him but that wasn't going to happen.

She awoke at dawn. The morning light glistened on the dew that had collected on the windowpanes. With each passing minute, the white stucco walls brightened to spotlight the scene about to unfold. Yet again, Leah mentally rehearsed the showdown with Javier.

"Let's get up," she suggested when he stirred beside her. "You're going on a hunt, and I'm returning to Madrid. I'll order room service."

"Okay, but how about this first?" He slid his leg between hers and nuzzled his face in her neck.

Leah turned her back to him, said nothing, got up and closed the bathroom door behind her. Was she closing him out of her life? She stepped into the shower's steamy mist, toweled off, dressed fully and returned to the room. When she looked into Javier's eyes, her throat knotted. She swallowed hard.

"What's up, Leah?"

"We need to talk."

No man wants to hear those words. Women present emotions and problems without boundaries. Men want solutions in a box. One, two, fixed. His face told her that he didn't want a serious conversation; he only wanted to offer the question. Dwelling on unpleasant issues wasn't his strong point.

"I'm done being your part-time lover again," she said. "You're now free to be with me full-time but you want a *communal life* making love to many women. What's up with that logic?"

Javier sat stunned at the side of the bed. He rubbed his chin, moistened his lips, lowered his head and sighed. "What would it be for us? A full-time but long-distance relationship means I'd go to New York and you'd come here. But I don't see you living in Spain. The cultural divide is too great. You don't speak Spanish that well."

"We'd work it out. I'd go to classes. Maybe we'd live full-time together in one location. I'd move to Spain if you wanted." He didn't answer her. Instead, she saw that faraway and disinterested look in his eyes. She knew they were finished.

"I don't want a commitment again, Leah. I want a casual, yet loving arrangement. Sometimes we're too old for all that life offers. You have a full and exciting life. I'm still mourning, with teenage children to raise. I don't want to leave Spain and live elsewhere, even temporarily. I don't know how to live with another woman or begin something steady with you."

"Coward. I so wanted a different answer. Did you ever love me deeply?" She was heartbroken and angry as tears welled in her eyes.

"Of course, I loved you and I continue to love you. In fact, more as the years pass. What a foolish question. I wouldn't be here if I didn't."

"What's missing is that your love was never deep enough. It wasn't real. I've grown to love me more as I age. What a disservice I did to myself by meeting you in this room."

She wanted to scream, tear at his eyes and spit at him. Instead, she sat beside him on their bed and removed his hands from his face. She leaned over and kissed his cheek. He didn't respond. She then left the bed, put her book in her small bag, zippered it shut and placed it beside the door. She removed her jacket from the closet and put it over her arm. Several taps on the door startled her. When she opened it, a hotel waiter stood ready to roll the breakfast cart into the room, complete with a red rose in a silver vase. Leah motioned for him to enter the deafening silence. After he left, she looked at Javier one last time. He remained on the bed with his underwear on, knees apart and with his hands holding his head.

"Please don't leave me," he said softly when he looked up.

"You're pathetic," she said, and slammed the door behind her.

~ ♡ ~

Leah walked to the bus station to clear her mind. How remarkably peaceful and deeply saddened she felt, simultaneously. But she had learned through the years that a relationship shifts as each partner jockeys for position. She and Javier met in a hotel lobby while she temporarily lived in Spain. He was the dashing Spaniard. She was a free-spirited American. They were lovers only; a couple incapable of adapting to their differences as time passed. If they were younger in that Salamanca hotel room, maybe they could have grown together. Now in their fifties, they only had memories. At least she knew where she stood with him. She'd never look back.

Leah scolded herself for all the wrong choices she'd made with men. Why did she prolong a bad love affair, hoping it would turn her way, especially when she recognized the early pitfalls? Was being a collector of affections her nature, an engrained trait? Could she be imitating the tale about the scorpion's nature that never changes?

"Mr. Frog," the scorpion said as she sat on the riverbed. "Will you carry me across?"

"No."

"Why not?"

"If I give you a ride on my back, you'll sting me, and I'll drown."

"But Mr. Frog, if I sting you, then I'll drown since I can't swim."

"You're right. Hop on," he said, and they entered the water. Halfway across, the scorpion stung the frog's back. As her poison raced through his veins, he looked back at her. "Why did you do that? You promised not to. Now we will both drown." "I'm sorry, Mr. Frog. But I couldn't help it. It's my nature."

Leah purchased her ticket to Madrid, waited in the downstairs bay for the bus to load and compared her behavior to the scorpion. She wasn't that bad. It couldn't be her nature to lure men into her web and kill them off with unrealistic expectations. Seeing Javier was a calculated risk; she lacked clear judgment to think they would become a committed couple. If she resumed the affair he envisioned, she'd suffer from that decision, stop smiling and be overwhelmed with shame. Absurd as it was, she'd need to assume a second or a third position. His work, his hunting, his Spanish friends, his children and other needs would come before her. Why do that when she wanted laughter, brilliant eyes, truth, peace, love, tenderness, open communication and fabulous, predictable lovemaking? She concluded that meeting him had been temporary insanity on her part. She'd never talk to him again. She'd never inflict self-damage again. The ill-fated rendezvous with Javier was a great lesson, hard but well learned. The time had come to create a more complete and honest life for herself.

Thoughts of a steady guy made her euphoric as the bus traveled along, stopping at villages to pick up new passengers. She'd find him some day. No more drama with men. "Dear God," she whispered, "if there really is a good man left on Earth to love and he'll love me unconditionally, please send him my way. I'm ready." Flashes of the Italian proverb she'd posted on her Internet home page appeared during the wish – *Below the navel there is neither religion nor truth.*

CHAPTER THREE

THE BUCOLIC AND PASTORAL SCENES en route to Madrid blurred as Leah's eyes drooped and finally closed after the exhausting visit with Javier combined with her lingering jet lag. When the bus jerked to a stop at the AutoRes station, she rubbed her eyes awake and was the last person to get off. Just being in the city again gave her an adrenaline high to walk the few blocks to the subway station where she swiped her multi-ride ticket at the turnstile. Tirso de Molina was her stop, close to the center of Madrid. Although familiar with the area, she still ran her finger over the subway platform map and counted the number of stations before she'd get off the train.

She exited the subway and walked the few blocks to her apartment building. She planned a good night's sleep. The next day she'd stroll her favorite streets. Fresh thinking and a much-needed sea change in her life were on the agenda. Leah adored Madrid. She acclimated quickly whenever she arrived; the city had remained in her heart long after her feet first touched its soil. First stop would be the Museo del Jamon restaurant for a *bocadillo doble* with *Jamon Serrano* and a beer. It wasn't a fancy place with hundreds of cured ham legs dangling from the ceiling but she liked mingling with the stand-up patrons. A visit to the Prado Museum was obligatory to view her favorite painting – Bosch's *The Garden of Earthly Delights* triptych. A small crowd usually formed in front of the oil masterpiece painted in the 1500s, which some interpreted as a depiction of the perils of life's temptations. Leah drew inspiration from the creativity of others, especially insightful paintings that told a larger story. She hoped to create equally beautiful scenes in her novels where exquisite surroundings, combined with challenges for her characters, filled page after page.

But as she neared her apartment building, she became increasingly despondent about being alone. Once inside the slow birdcage-elevator that inched upward, she was disgusted with herself over the Javier reunion. She flipped open her cell phone and scrolled to his name. "Here's to the death of good intentions," she said and deleted his number, pressing harder than necessary.

Leah went straight to the bedroom when she entered the apartment and pulled at an overhead chain to light the ceiling fixture. Her large suitcase was on the bed with the airline's luggage tag still looped around the handle. Many older Madrid apartments didn't have closets. Instead, an ornate walnut armoire stood across the room, sturdy on its clawed wrought-iron feet. She turned the antique key and the doors squeaked open. She hung up what she could and crammed smaller items into the bottom drawer.

When it finally occurred to her that the bedroom was too dark for the bright Spanish morning, she opened the red velvet drapes and rolled up the outside metal shutter. She didn't hear her cell phone ring until the room had brightened. How odd. Not many people had her Spanish number. Checking the caller

ID, no name appeared, only a sequence of nine numbers. She hesitated, trying to remember the last four digits of Javier's phone. When she was convinced it wasn't a call from him, she answered.

"Welcome back, Leah. Recognize this voice?" the male caller asked.

"Well hello, seatmate Miguel," she said, trying not to gush and reveal her delight. What a wonderful surprise to hear your voice. So you didn't forget me?"

"Forget you? Never. I've thought about you ever since you left for Salamanca. How'd it go, by the way?" he said but didn't wait for her response. Instead, he continued about his day at the Prado Museum, made all the more wonderful with a personal guide who highlighted the fourteen must-see masterpieces. Miguel then paused, leaving Leah to anticipate his next sentence. "You up for a flamenco show with me tonight?"

If she told the truth, she wasn't up for anything but a slow walk around Madrid, a solitary dinner at a restaurant with an outside terrace, people watching, some fine Spanish wine and a good night's sleep.

"Of course I'll go. I love flamenco. It will be great to see you again."

Leah remembered how he had intrigued her on the plane – enough to keep her talking until the Spanish dawn. He made her feel alive. She became a young girl enchanted with his flirting despite their middle-aged hearts. Well, maybe it wasn't flirting. She wanted it to be. Whatever it was, it was magic. She wanted more. He'd be a fun distraction after the brutal reality of Javier.

It was a short walk from her apartment to the Puerta del Sol where she'd meet Miguel under the clock tower. Should she tell him about Javier? Probably not since she might cry. Maybe he'd forget to ask her again. Leah was a strong woman and could discuss practically anything with anybody but she preferred to forget the Salamanca event.

"There you are. You look wonderful," Miguel said after he maneuvered through a small crowd to greet Leah.

His hug thrilled her. A whiff of cologne trailed as he brushed his smooth cheeks against hers with two kisses that escaped into the air. What an infectious and upbeat attitude he had.

"Before we go to the *tablao*, let's have a quick bite. I discovered a terrific tapas place on my way to meet you."

"How about we go to the Museo del Jamon? It's a block away. I'm due for my first *bocadillo* in Madrid. Agree?" He did.

"You seem a little off," Miguel said as they walked along. "Is everything okay?"

"I'm fine. Just pensive, which I can be sometimes," she said and led him into the restaurant, pointing out the deli selections and dangling cured ham legs.

Leah loved flamenco. Miguel hadn't seen the dance performed live nor did he know much about its origin. As they sat at a small table close to the stage, she explained that flamenco's birthplace was Costa del Sol, the region running the length of the Spain's southern coast. Many of the dancers were descended from Gypsy families. They'd been coded at birth to understand flamenco's language and music. The only requisite needed for the rest of the world to experience this exquisite art form was a passion for flamenco's beauty, sorrow and pain.

"How do you know so much?" Miguel asked as the *tablao* filled with animated patrons.

"When I lived in Spain years ago, I'd go to Andalucia to see flamenco performed by the pros. I'm a true devotee. This was the perfect invite for me tonight."

She then explained flamenco's three elements: the song, which was most important; the dancers, and the music, primarily guitarists. The clapping hands of the performers, who sat onstage in a row of simple, rustic chairs, were the magical accompaniment to the flamenco dancers' feet. The tapping in flamenco music imitated the sounds made in a forge. Many Andalucian men worked as blacksmiths. The lyrics sung during flamenco were often impromptu and composed on stage.

"If you give me your scent, I will give you my soul. How's that for sexy? It's the best I've heard," Leah told Javier.

Before he could answer, the lights dimmed and several guitar players sauntered on stage followed by six women dancers. Each flung a fringed shawl over one shoulder. The women had jet-black hair slicked back into a bun, highlighted with a red flower tucked behind one ear. "*Olé*," some audience members shouted as the dancers' castanets found their beat alongside the plucked guitars.

After the show, Miguel and Leah strolled in the midnight mist until they reached the city's Plaza Mayor, a massive main square like Salamanca's dating back centuries. It felt so right and so peaceful as he motioned for them to sit under a table umbrella and enjoy a nightcap.

"This is none of my business, and you can tell me that, but what happened with Javier in Salamanca?" Miguel asked when he stopped raving about the beauty around them.

"Our blissful rendezvous was a disaster. He wants me as a quasi-companion, an occasional lover. He still grieves for his deceased wife and wants to be a full-time and unattached widower with children."

"So what did you say?"

"I wanted us to be a committed couple."

"And?"

"It's not going to happen. I'll never see or talk to him again. And to think all those years we've known one another went poof. I'll miss the friendship. Oh well."

"I didn't expect that answer."

"You're a guy with good instincts. Why did he want me for so long and then reject me? I know he loves me but not enough."

"*La familia* is exceptionally important to Spaniards. It can withstand a lot. You can kiss him good-bye if he brought his family into the picture. Ask yourself if you want to get involved in that scenario for a lifetime. His wife's memory and their children will always come before you."

"Is it also cultural differences? He brought that up."

"That, too, but mostly he lacks courage when it comes to women. I know many men in Spain like Javier and even some in America. How others perceive them and their marriage is important. He loves you. I'm sure of that. But don't expect him to change. You're too independent for him."

"I wasn't before. Why did he remarry his ex-wife?"

"They probably had an odd marriage but, in his own way, he loved her. Forget him, Leah. He won't live the life you need. I'm a Spaniard, too, but I've lived in America long enough to appreciate a woman like you. Forget Javier."

His insight startled her. Before she could respond, strolling *La Tuna* musicians stopped at their table to serenade them. The minstrel group recreated a twelfth-century tradition begun when struggling university students supported themselves through donations given by appreciative listeners. The group still dressed in traditional costume: black jackets with slashed sleeves; black calf-length or shorter trousers; black tights and shoes, complemented with a white shirt and a colored sash representing the wearer's college. When they left their table to serenade another couple, Miguel suggested it was time to leave. "What a beautiful night, Leah," he said, and reached for her hand.

They lingered outside her apartment building. She wanted to invite him in but resisted the impulse. Instead, she wished him well in his travels through Castilla y Leon and Castilla-LaMancha that would begin the next morning. He'd be gone for two weeks and fly back to Virginia without stopping in Madrid again.

"Call me from the road if you remember. I'd love to hear your impressions of Spain," Leah said in parting.

"How about breakfast tomorrow before I drive to Segovia? Maybe you can give me some travel tips," he said hesitantly.

"I'd love that. You know about the aqueduct in Segovia. Right? Oh, and be sure to eat lamb or roasted pig. I'll think of some more things," she said, elated at his request to see her again.

~ ♡ ~

"Have you seen Segovia?" Miguel asked Leah at the end of their breakfast.

"Yes. Beautiful place."

"Want to see it again?" he said softly.

"Now?" she asked incredulously. She'd seen the famed city with the Roman aqueduct several times, but she accepted his offer with excitement.

What was going on? Her emails would be left to languish; her pledge to write, sabotaged; her friends neglected and long walks abandoned. Instead, she'd spend the day in Segovia with tender Miguel. He'd later reveal how his invitation had become a struggle when Susan, his Virginia girlfriend, flashed across his thoughts. He invited Leah anyway.

"Seatmates again. Destination Segovia," Miguel said as they buckled their car seatbelts. "Happy to have you aboard, madam," he added and saluted.

Once on the road, Spain's magnificent and billboard-free highway opened up before them with panoramic views of the Meseta, the massive central plateau in the center of the Iberian Peninsula. At times, stark brown and gray tones highlighted the parched earth. Square bales of khaki-colored hay were piled into stair-like forms while others were placed randomly on the farmlands. It was a delightful ride.

The conversation included his favorite literary characters, many names new to Leah. Mostly they laughed and shared anecdotes from their lives. But there was more going on than conversation, and they knew it. They were well-schooled in the art of seduction and its consequences. When they ran away to Segovia, Miguel broke his commitment to a trusting woman back home. Leah betrayed her, too, though neither of them mentioned that.

Despite being successful business people with a few gray hairs, they acted like carefree teenagers, stretching each hour to its fullest. They arrived in glorious Segovia in the afternoon. Absorbing it all, they sat at an outdoor cafe in a cozy, embracing plaza where stone buildings were adorned with wrought-iron balconies covered with geraniums.

As the day slipped into early evening, they strolled arm

in arm, stopping often to laugh along the stone streets and to window shop. Miguel had a comedic sense of timing and would act out dramatic parts. One moment he'd be a boisterous, angry Spaniard jamming his hand into the bend of his elbow. Then he'd drop his voice several octaves and become a gravel-voiced old man.

Rounding a corner, they came upon Segovia's multi-spire, sixteenth-century cathedral where the spotlights illuminated and spilled into the Plaza Mayor and over its ornate wrought-iron bandstand. Absorbed by the beauty of the city, Miguel and Leah missed the tolling of the Town Hall's hourly bell. When they finally checked bus and train schedules, it was too late for her to return to Madrid.

"How about we have dinner in Segovia? I'll change my double-bed room for one with two singles. You can return to Madrid in the morning," Miguel suggested.

"Sure. That sounds like a good plan," she said hesitantly.

The reality was that she didn't have a quick answer and didn't know what to do. His *two single beds* suggestion made her feel a little trapped. Being intimate with Miguel wasn't what she had in mind. She assumed he didn't either. Nothing about their day hinted at romance. His hotel invite didn't have a sexual nuance; otherwise, she'd have opted for her own room. She had made love with Javier in Salamanca and wasn't ready to make love to a different man so soon afterward. And it wasn't her style to be coerced into a suggestion like his. She was too worldly for that nonsense. She couldn't imagine he'd be so naïve to think she'd sleep with him. They were new friends, seatmate buddies now in Spain. She liked it that way.

But resisting Miguel's charm had become difficult for her, especially when he spoke to Spaniards in their language. He sounded so gallant and polished. She listened and smiled as he stopped a sweet, arm-holding pair of elderly women to ask for their perfect restaurant suggestion. The evening had a cool nighttime breeze. Leah's arm was linked into his, and she pressed closer to feel his warmth. The women's choice was the nearby José María Restaurant. It had a four-foot-wide, cast-iron suckling pig on its outside wall lying in a roasting pan with its head and legs hanging over the rim. Skilled waiters could cut through the regional *cochinillo asado* dish by making blunt cuts with a dinner plate turned sideways.

Miguel and Leah were led to a back table. Hundreds of wine bottlenecks, some covered in dust, protruded from an aqueduct-style wine rack attached to the wall. Black-suited waiters scurried about with white napkins draped over one arm, matching the tablecloths draped on the tables. Talavera de la Reina ceramic *artesania* wall plates encircled a photo of Spain's King Juan Carlos shaking hands with the restaurant owner. And while the crowd buzzed with animated talk, Miguel and Leah spoke softer and sweeter words as the hours passed and the wine flowed.

"I love your face and eyes," he said. "I really like you a lot, Leah."

"Beautiful compliments, Miguel. Don't stop them."

"Can you believe we're having dinner in Segovia? When I sat next to you on that plane, my trip didn't include this night with you. Every day had a purpose; every night had a hotel room for one."

"Hey, sometimes we get sprinkled with magic dust when we travel. Maybe that's what happened. Celebrate life. We're living the best of it right now."

Leah fed Miguel from her plate, tracing her lips with her

tongue. The long, enchanting dinner ended with a nightcap, compliments of their waiter. As they left the restaurant, Leah realized she'd never intended to find herself falling in love with Miguel – never – but under the stars, a teasing moon beckoned them to their hotel, a short walk along a street lined with vintage hitching posts.

Arriving at Room 104 became a blur in her memory. Her first clear recollection was of stepping out of the hot shower with her nipples erect. Since she didn't have a nightgown, she borrowed Miguel's T-shirt and pulled up her lace panties for the walk to her twin bed. She had a crucial decision to make about the intense desire that was heating and moistening her as intensely as the shower had done. She decided to share her confusion.

"Miguel," she called, as she opened the bathroom door. He approached wearing a T-shirt and shorts. "I'm confused. I don't know what to do. We've had a wonderful day. I don't want it to end. Now we're alone in this room. What will happen to us if we make love?"

"Here's my answer," he said and placed her hand on his hidden erection.

"I thought so," she whispered as they kissed briefly at the bathroom door before she pulled away. She walked into the bedroom with the two single beds and chose the one closest to the wall. Miguel stood in the shadows watching her.

"I want you," she sighed when their eyes met.

He walked slowly over to her bed, lay down beside her and slipped one arm under her neck while the other drew her closer to him. They murmured endearing words on their shared pillow, words that neither had said aloud. When their naked bodies touched, it was the inevitable continuation of their minds connecting on the plane. His first kisses were short and awkward, like those of a schoolboy's. The window shutters were slightly ajar, and the golden light reflecting into their room from the nineteen-century outdoor lantern was their bed cover. If the room was cold, they didn't notice. Words vanished as their kisses intensified.

"*Te adoro*, Leah," he whispered as his tongue moistened her ear. "I adore you," he repeated in English. "What is happening to us?"

"I don't know," she sighed.

He cupped her head with his gentle hands, met her eyes with his, smiled his love for her and then gently slid his tongue inside her mouth that he had squeezed into a tight opening. She accepted it and pushed her body against his, returning his passion. His moist tongue encircled her nipples, eventually moving down her body until she could see his adoring eyes gazing up at her from between her legs. Miguel was a superb lover, a giver.

"This changes everything," she gasped, as he tasted a different Leah.

When he raised her legs to inch himself over her, he rubbed his erection against the wetness between her legs. The only sound she heard as he found his way inside her was the flow of her own sweet juices assuring Miguel he was finally home that night. When she rolled on top of him, his fingers stroked her hips. Later, she caressed his thighs, gently spreading them so her lips could take him into her mouth.

"You know what you're doing," he moaned and whispered. "You're an eighteenth-century courtesan." Leah jokingly asked if an eighteenth-century courtesan translated into a modern-day whore.

"Not at all. You're beautiful, intelligent, and you love to make love. You've been made love to very well."

It was a supreme compliment. A gold medal bestowed to her on a pedestal of sheets. She imagined the sensuous women of years passed who loved the noblemen in the books Miguel carried in his head and heart.

"One man would never have been enough for you," he said as Leah climaxed.

When he drifted off to sleep, she lay awake shaking her head against the pillow. What had she done? What had they done? And what would come next?

Spain's nightlife is infamous and Segovia's youth lived up to its reputation through the wee hours of the morning. Young women on clicking high heels and rowdy young men paraded beneath their semi-opened windows as Miguel slept. Leah didn't. The Calle de Isabel la Católica stone walkway below honored Spain's fifteenth-century queen who financed Christopher Columbus' journey to the New World. Was Leah about to take a new journey with Miguel? How did their lovemaking happen so fast? She'd just broken away from a man she'd wanted to be her lifetime companion. Miguel had a girlfriend at home. Maybe the alcohol at dinner had lowered their resistance. Maybe hot, sexy Spain enticed them into bed. Or maybe not. Her single life had its merits, but what was she doing in bed with a seatmate she'd just met?

"Let's make love again," he suggested when he awoke slowly and reached for Leah just as the phone rang. "Don't answer that," he said quickly and sat upright. His request was too late as her hello passed through the receiver.

"It was my wake-up call. Don't you remember I'm taking the bus back to Madrid this morning?" she said when she hung up. An all-too-familiar sensation came over her as she saw Miguel staring straight ahead. A committed man in another woman's bed is terrified if he thinks he's been caught. "It's quarter past two in the morning in Virginia. Your girlfriend is probably asleep in your bed, and you're in mine," Leah said.

"I don't want you to go," he said pulling her close as he placed his erection between her legs. The night had transformed them into instantaneous and moist lovers, which again placed him inside her with ease. His lustful climax came from a place in his heart, body and soul that had lain dormant for years. The Spanish words he gasped between gritted teeth called out to the deities in the heavens.

"I haven't cum in Spanish for years," he said and slumped to one side of their bed.

~ ♡ ~

Riding the stuffy bus to Madrid sickened Leah. The rushed breakfast coffee and pastry she shared with Miguel curdled in her stomach. The abundance of wine the night before created a pounding headache. She placed her forehead against the cool windowpane as the crowded bus bounced along. How did a simple invitation to Segovia result in an overnight with Miguel, being hung over and so sexually aroused with his memory that she was still moist? She wasn't that impetuous to run off willy-nilly with a stranger but that's exactly what she did. She was a seasoned woman with an attuned instinct for choosing lasting bedmates and not one-night stands. Her Madrid trip was supposed to resolve issues that gnawed at her psyche, not create new ones. But what incredible joy Miguel gave her.

When the bus pulled into the Madrid bus station, Leah had already been in and out of the city twice despite being in

Spain for only four days. She'd contacted none of her Madrid friends or her family back home. The refrigerator was empty; her emails unanswered. She was flat out exhausted, physically and emotionally. She'd slept with two men and neither was permanently at her side.

Leah's apartment building with its balconies overlooking a green plaza and a gushing fountain was a welcomed sight. Once inside, she went directly to the bedroom, lowered the metal shutters, took a shower, slid naked under the bed covers and slept for the entire day.

"I need to talk to you right away," Leah said to her friend Rocío. It was the first call she made when she woke up. She was still in bed when she reached for the phone.

"Welcome to Madrid, Leah. Or should I say welcome home. Where are you? I lost your cell number and was getting nervous when you didn't call."

"Oh my God, Rocío. The most amazing thing happened. I don't know why I did it. Can I see you in an hour?"

"Of course but give me a hint. You always have a story. This one sounds extra special."

"Hint? Think seatmate, Segovia, lust and confusion."

"What? Oh, never mind. Come visit me. I'll make *paella*. I know, I know, no shrimp for you, only chicken. Hurry."

"Great. I'll bring the wine."

Refreshed and eager to see her friend, Leah dressed quickly and took a cab to the wealthy Salamanca district and Rocío's apartment on Calle de Lagasca. The building had a *potero* who opened the door for her, modern elevators and slick marble hallways. Rocío had decorated her spacious two-bedroom home with exquisite taste. Leah adored her friend but not her cats. The friends had remained in frequent contact that evolved with Skype and email. A favorite topic was men.

"*Guapa*," Rocío greeted Leah as she opened the door with a flourish. "You look marvelous. Come in, come in," she repeated after they rocked back and forth in a bear hug. "Let's uncork your wine and you can tell me your fantastic story. Or should I only ask his name? Wait, don't tell me just yet. First we need full wine glasses. Wow! Look at that smile on your face."

Leah walked out onto Rocío's terrace while her friend prepared their drinks. Any skyline view was limited since the apartment was located in a congested neighborhood. Instead, she peered over the railing, remembering the many times Javier treated her to shopping sprees on the upscale street below.

"Okay, my dear, begin," Rocío said when she joined Leah, and they toasted. "Who's the mystery man?"

"Miguel Santiago," Leah said and blew out his name between pursed lips. "He was my seatmate on the flight over. We talked the entire way. I never expected to see him again, but we ran away to Segovia where we made love. It's incredible this happened to me. Javier and I slept together in Salamanca, too, but we're finished. Completely finished."

"You're talking too fast, Leah. Slow down, please. I can't follow you. One lover at a time."

Rocío never took her gaze away from Leah, sitting stone-faced as a cat jumped on her lap. She still had a shapely body with narrow hips, rounded breasts and long legs. Her flawless skin contrasted with her jet-black hair pulled back in a bun with an exotic Spanish comb tucked in it. Her expensive clothes came from the top shops on Calle Serrano accented with scarves purchased at Loewe. Rocío wore 18-karat gold bracelets and Majorica pearls.

She was also a seasoned woman so Leah felt at ease discussing her sexual escapades of the past few days. Although her friend had had several romances in and out of marriage, she'd soured with age and was judgmental.

"Listen. Javier is like most men," Rocío said. "He didn't want an emotional conflict with you and took the line of least resistance. He reverted to what was comfortable and familiar behavior. You were his mistress, even after his wife's death."

"So you don't like affairs. Is that what you're saying? Or no affairs with married men or Spanish men with deceased wives?" Leah questioned a bit annoyed with her friend.

"You should only be involved with single men who want a new woman. Learn from my mistakes, Leah. Don't you remember the delirious and painful affair I had with Ricardo?" He was a fellow Spaniard, married to a Spanish woman and lived in New York. He and Rocío were lovers when she was married and living in New York. "I'm still disgraced behind my back and hurting. We were deeply in love. But when our affair was discovered, I lost my husband, his wealth, my standing in the Spanish community and self-respect. Ricardo only lost me."

"And guess what?" Rocío asked Leah. She tried to laugh but tears came instead. "Ricardo and his wife are still married with memories of a long life together, me being one of them. My husband and I *separated* for years until Spanish law let us divorce. Would I have had the affair if I had known the outcome? No. I should have known better. I'm a Spaniard but love and lust have no conscience. *La familia*, Spanish marriages, infidelities and no divorce are an engrained way of life for some of us."

"Did I do the right thing by leaving Javier?" Leah asked.

"Absolutely. Why ask me that? You know you did. Move on. You deserve better. Now tell me about Miguel. This one might have some promise."

"Truthfully, you may not like this story," she said and relived the plane ride and Segovia. "He's incredible. What a charmer. What a lover. I'm crazy about him. It was lust for sure but something else was going on. He's got a girlfriend in Virginia."

"Oh, come on, Leah. A girlfriend back home?" Rocío said and looked down her nose, shrugging her shoulder. "Not nice behavior for the two of you?"

"I know, I know. But he's not engaged or married. She sounds like a sister or best friend. For me, it was sexy and perfect timing after the dump from Javier. I don't expect to see Miguel again. I just wanted your reaction to this far-fetched seatmate story. So what's your advice on affairs? What should I do?"

"Truthfully? I think lustful love where you lose your sense of direction is a sickness. Avoid it. Cultivate deep friendship, then make love but not when either party is involved with someone else. The relationship works better without a lie as the foundation. Miguel will be back. Mark my words. But let's forget men for now and eat *paella*. I prefer to hear about your family and your daughter's wedding plans," Rocío said as she took the wine glass out of Leah's hand and led her to the kitchen.

CHAPTER FOUR

A TRIP TO MADRID WASN'T COMPLETE for Leah without a visit to El Corte Inglés, the country's largest department store chain. After her visit with Rocío, she stopped in and filled her cart with *Manchego* cheese, *chorizo,* Marcona almonds, bread still warm to the touch, mixed olives and microwave meals. At the checkout line, a muffled cell phone ring went unanswered until she realized it came from her purse.

"I'm baaaaaack," Miguel said with a chuckle when she answered.

"So you are. I can't talk right now. Can I call you back?"

"Sure. It's the hotel in Segovia. Room 104. Hopefully you remember what happened to us there. Miss you lots."

Leah wished for wheels on her feet as she hurried home. Once inside, she put her shopping bags on the kitchen counter, poured herself a glass of red wine and dialed the Segovia hotel. At the sound of Miguel's voice, she inhaled deeply and envisioned them in bed.

"I adore Segovia," he said. He had stayed an extra day to walk the city, returning to the hotel with blisters on his feet and sunburn on his nose. He had lunch at a landmark restaurant under the famed aqueduct, eating slowly, needing to assess what had happened to him since he met Leah. "I'm really troubled about that night. It's not you. It's me. I feel so guilty. Susan trusts me when I travel alone. How could I have broken that trust?" His voice trailed off.

"We were swept away by the entire day, which led to an incredible night of lovemaking. I can't stop thinking about it, but I'm not guilty. I wish you didn't live with someone."

They talked at length, agreeing that if either were married, they wouldn't have done it. A love affair between two single people is one thing. But he wasn't totally single. It wasn't adultery either. But what happened wasn't right.

"You may find this hard to believe but I'm a monogamous man. It takes a lot of mental energy and deceit to lie to someone. When I'm in a relationship, I'm in it full time. I've traveled alone before and what happened with you is a first."

"I'm feeling used right now. Did we have a quickie in Segovia and is this a goodbye call? If yes, let's move on alone. We're not teenagers; we're in our fifties. I don't regret our night. I'm just confused. Damn it, I keep saying 'confused' because I don't know what else to call the emotion. You abducted me with that ride to Segovia. Then you seduced me. You're in the boat with me now."

"I miss you so much, Leah. I want you with me all the time," he said. "How about we meet in Salamanca tomorrow? I'll be in the same hotel you stayed in with Javier. Will that upset you? We can meet in the lobby."

"I can meet you there. I want to see you again, too."

"Great. I'll pick up a few CDs for our drive into the Wine Region. We'll spend the day and night there. What the hell. Shall we roll the dice while we're in Spain and go for it?"

"Sure. But don't forget this is only a made-in-Spain romance."

When the call finished, Leah sat in the overstuffed living room chair with the floral print and shook her head in disbelief. She baffled herself. Why was she running off with a man who offered a zero future as a couple? He was only good for a few days of giggles, hugs, great lovemaking and tenderness. She wanted a free man. She wanted a commitment. Someone special to take to her daughter's wedding. But something within told her to follow her heart, not her pessimistic head.

She wanted to call Rocío with the Miguel news. But she figured her friend might squelch the joy. Instead, she spent a quiet evening surfing websites about Spain's Wine Region. She called her children to say she'd landed in Madrid. Dana was out, probably wedding-day shopping, so Leah left a message. No need to mention Miguel to her. The dalliance was silly. She didn't need to be reminded.

Two Salamanca visits in one week with two different men disturbed Leah as the bus pulled into the station. It was unsettling. The walking route to the hotel was the same one she followed to meet Javier. She again marveled at the medieval buildings and heard the storks cluck and the church bells chime. *How weird is this?* What was Miguel thinking? Leah wasn't feeling at all nonchalant as she entered the hotel lobby. She was extremely uncomfortable. Miguel was scanning the tourist rack. He seemed hesitant when he greeted her with the customary kiss on each cheek.

"Let's take a walk through Salamanca before we begin our long drive," she said, hoping to lessen the uneasiness. She took his hand while he reached in his jacket with the other and pulled out his pocket-sized guidebook. As each block passed, their pace slowed to a more leisurely stroll until they reached a small Renaissance patio, part of Salamanca University where the Escuelas Menores was located. Many centuries ago, graduating students wrote their initials on the building in ink made from bull's blood mixed with olive oil and herbs.

"Look closely at the carvings. See if you can find the frog on a skull," Miguel said and pointed to the guidebook photo. "You will be assured success in several areas of your life if you find it."

Leah liked the one where a woman would find her mate, but she couldn't find the frog.

"Let's translate this," she said and stopped Miguel next to an inscription on another building. *Primero la verdad, que la paz.*

"First truth, then peace," they said in unison.

"Agree?" Leah asked. Miguel didn't respond.

"Tell me about Susan," she said "Shouldn't you be with her today and not with me?"

"I'll tell you about all the women. It's a long list. I wanted Susan to be the last woman I'd make love to but I may have made a mistake when I asked her to move in. Something big is missing, but I think I'm too old to find it elsewhere. Are you ready for my story?" he asked and led Leah to an outdoor café in the Plaza Mayor.

"Begin," she said softly when they found a table in the sun.

Some men don't attract women; Miguel drew them in like a magnet. He adored their scent, their lilting laughter and their sensuous bodies that welcomed him inside theirs, squeezing every bit of indifference out of him. He believed nothing compared to a man and woman making love. Nothing.

"I love you," he'd said to many women in his twenties and meant it. As he looked deeply into their eyes and whispered the secrets of their bed, he instinctively recognized his moment of conquest when their shoulders dropped just slightly. He never considered himself a ladies' man; he simply loved women. As he sailed through his thirties and forties, his gifts to women grew in value as he became a wealthy man with the family business. His homes upgraded from a messy one-bedroom apartment to a luxurious three-bedroom home with a housekeeper and a gardener. His furnishings, once purchased at second-hand stores, now included a sumptuous leather living room set, Oriental rugs and valuable accessories. The interior of his Mercedes in the driveway smelled new because it was, every year.

In his early thirties, he married Joanne, self-consciously aware that people questioned his extended bachelorhood. An older man advised marrying someone slim and clean because in time she'd become fat and dirty. Joanne was a sweet girl, small in stature and a good cook. What is love, he thought, but a fleeting emotion. Sex was an endless mystery. He always needed it, and it was always available.

Marriage quickly turned into an obligation that he couldn't fulfill. Joanne's expectations of what he should be didn't match his. He was faithful to her, although he admired other women. She miscarried early in their marriage. Potential fatherhood shocked him into realizing it would be more difficult to leave her if the next pregnancy succeeded. He'd already fallen out of love. Everyone else loved her but he didn't anymore. On Valentine's Day, he couldn't fake a romantic dinner and told her the marriage was over.

Then there was Shannon, an advertising executive, with long red tresses. She was spirited, smoked a cigar at parties to horrify the other women and wore stilettos to set off her long legs. She hooked him immediately by the incredible way she took him in her mouth. He'd forever crave that skill in other women. They lasted a year before she ran off with a polo player from Brazil.

Monica followed Shannon. She and Miguel lived together for several years. They almost married until she told him about the large country house she envisioned filled with their children. He wasn't ready for that commitment. They ended with a hug, a handshake, her sobs, a friendship and a $15,000 check from him to help her start a new life. He remembered her most for their all-night trysts that included bondage and sex toys.

Laura followed Monica. She was cerebral. They met at a conference in Chicago, one he attended to bring the family business into the cyber world. They enjoyed lavish dinners where they discussed opera, the classics and modern art. On their bed, they traveled to a special planet where body, mind and soul melded. He enjoyed the fine tone of her body; every inch molded at the gym. But she lived in San Francisco, and he didn't. They had a magnificent, cross-country romance until the realities of missed flights, lonely weekends and sheer distance ended a love he wanted to last forever. She left him for a hometown lawyer. Miguel missed her intellect most and yearned for it in other women.

After Laura, he lived alone for several years, dated sporadically and wondered if his best years were over. Where was that special woman to soothe his aching heart? Had he stayed too long at the fair? He was aging, something he noticed daily. His skin drooped where it hadn't before. His constant sexual desire for women had waned. He'd become the old buck who walked down the hill to mate, compared to the younger muscle-quivering stallion galloping down at the slightest whiff of a female. Perhaps this slower pace was a disguised blessing.

The family business consumed most of his time. He lived like a wealthy man and immersed himself in following new modern-art painters. On occasion, he'd bed Julia, a young artist. She liked to tickle him between his legs using a paintbrush with fine bristles. He bought many of her abstract over-sized paintings but gave them away.

Miguel met Susan in an art gallery. She and a group of friends had decided to expand their worlds that day and try new things. They lunched on escargot and foie gras in a French bistro, ordered the most expensive Pinot Noir and topped off the afternoon at the gallery. Viewing paintings up close was new to Susan. She'd married young and assumed a mundane stay-at-home life as a housewife and mother not drawn to cultural events. After her divorce, she vowed to expand her small world.

Simply by chance, she and Miguel found themselves admiring a Jackson Pollock painting. Conversation was easy. Normally, she avoided strange men but his smile charmed her. She had lived a celibate life for ten years, focusing only on her children. Susan was sweet. That's what prompted Miguel to ask if he could call her. He was ready for a sweet woman. He was ready for a woman who lived in the same city. A woman with children took the pressure off him to produce a child with her.

They dated casually at first and waited several months to make love. She was a telephone company supervisor with a small bank account, no passport and drove a second-hand car. He introduced Susan to frilly camisoles, pink garter belts and sex toys. She accepted the lingerie but was uneasy learning new sexual positions and touching the erotic toys. Eventually, he gave up trying to elevate and educate her desire and settled for the missionary position. After countless years of angst over break-ups, dramas, a broken marriage and failed love affairs, Susan offered Miguel a stability that matched his age and his wants although she never recognized his needs. After a few years of consistent dating, he purchased yet another home. Her shoulders dropped when he asked her to move in. He heard her breathless yes before she said it. Their combined furniture was barely in place when he packed for his solo trip to Spain with her blessing.

After their farewell kiss at the Virginia airport that fall afternoon, Miguel ran his tongue across her lips. He promised to call her. When he landed in New York to connect with the flight to Spain, an immense feeling of freedom washed over him. Walking through the terminal, he was jubilant. Two weeks to be himself and sleep alone. Two weeks to speak his native language and be a European again.

"I wasn't in my seat more than two minutes when the flight attendant tapped my shoulder," Miguel said to Leah as they sat in Salamanca. "Would you mind changing your seat with another passenger?" she asked. "So I move back several rows, click my seatbelt shut and meet Leah Lynch, a woman who's turning my heart and world upside down right now."

Leah never once interrupted his story. When he finished, she gave him a questioning look.

"Wow. Lots of women and fleeting commitments. Want me to be blunt?"

"Yes."

"Sounds like you react best to *receiving* love and reject *giving* it in its purest form for an extended time. This happens to some men who begin life as the *object* of their mother's love. She smothers her son from birth and unwittingly stunts his relationships with other women. So he moves through adolescence and into manhood always taking, and expecting, love from women. Plus, any woman's love would never measure up to what he'd felt from his mother's love. That's all he knows. It's his nature. But a normal man-woman relationship gives love to both people."

"Am I that screwed up? Are you saying I'm a teenager? I sure as hell feel like one sometimes."

"I'm not a shrink but something's wrong here. That theory is Freudian-based. It makes sense. It takes years for some men to stop dumping women and recognize their arrested development in the love category. It's a long and winding road for them to go from many women to just one, but they must do it alone. Blessed are those who come to that realization early in life. And thanks for sharing this part of your story with me. I know you better now."

"You're welcome. I know the chapters by heart. So it's a process? Let me think about that," he said.

"I'm working on the *process*, too," she said and reached for his hand. "Let's go back to the car. We have miles to travel before nightfall."

They buckled in for their ride to the province's renowned Ribera del Duero wine region where they'd overnight in El Burgo de Osma. A road map and CDs were slid into the door's pocket on his side and Leah's bag with its two-day wardrobe was in the back seat. The next day they'd drive to Siguenza and have lunch in its majestic parador. They were vague about an overnight for Leah. Before Miguel backed out of the parking space, he put his right arm behind her head and rested it on the back of her seat. He kissed her gently and looked into her eyes. "You have beautiful eyes, Leah."

"They like what they see right now," she whispered through the kiss.

He turned his body to face the steering wheel, shifted gears, backed out, inched down the driveway and pulled into traffic. Miguel and Leah left Salamanca, each with a different memory. His visit had a virginal quality – a man with his first encounter in the city. Hers was tinged with memories – a woman with history between her legs.

Their road trip through Spain's Castilla y Leon province began on a glorious sunny day. Leah opened a regional map on her lap that boasted more than half of the country's historic and artistic patrimony, plus the largest number of UNESCO World Heritage sites. With approximately three hundred castles built from the eighth to sixteenth centuries, she knew they'd pass by several. These former vestiges of battle had become romantic symbols; some had turned into hotels. They were all perfect backdrops because she was truly Miguel's queen riding beside him as he sang to her, created musical sounds with his wonderful mouth or tapped out songs on the steering wheel.

"I really like you, Leah," he said after a noticeable silence with the emphasis on *really*.

And she *really* liked him.

The two-lane highway passed by Spain's infamous stone pine trees with their short trunks and upturned pine-needle branches. They reminded her of wine glasses waiting for a pour. Some wineries had corrugated-metal rooftops and an industrial look, not interesting enough for a visit. One sign, however, advertised an eight-hundred-year-old winery.

"Let's see what this one is about," Miguel said and made a quick turn down a dirt road, stopping at the building's entrance. A sleepy dog jumped up, ran to the car and barked up at the window, wagging its tail.

"Hola, bienvenidos," said the jovial owner with the burly mustache, running down the stone steps. He called the dog to his side and welcomed Leah and Miguel to an impromptu tour of his wine cellar. *"Americanos?"* he asked as he led the way with a wide sweep of his arm. Miguel answered in Spanish saying he was born in Spain but had immigrated to America during his teenage years. To be greeted as a couple didn't go unnoticed by Leah.

The trio descended a long, narrow staircase and walked through dank, underground caves where the sweet aroma of fermentation filled their nostrils. Overhead, a thick mold clung to the vaulted ceiling, making the tour feel a bit ghoulish. Long rows of oak barrels, many made in France and America, filled the narrow passageways from floor to ceiling. Dates were scrawled on them with white chalk. Miguel translated for Leah.

"My local grapes produce the Chanel No. 5 of wines," the winemaker said at the end of the tour. He poured several glasses of a robust red. They should look for it on the menu of any parador in the country. Leah scribbled the name in her notebook and assured him they'd order it since their trip included a parador.

At the second winery they visited, now armed with more knowledge about the winemaking process, the owner told them the property belonged to his wife's family; the grapes came from his ancestors. The combination resulted in an excellent wine. He led Miguel and Leah several floors below to the "catacombs," as he referred to the cement building that housed his wines. Bach's "Requiem" filled the air.

"Our family's philosophy encourages us to combine art, culture and wine," the winemaker said in perfect English. He pointed to his line drawings of castles displayed on an easel beside the tanks. He too poured wine samples.

"Sip it," Leah said to Miguel. "We've got some driving to do. You need to be sober."

On the way out, Miguel purchased several bottles from the winemaker's tiny shop. "We travel well together," he said when he accompanied Leah to their car and held the door open for her. "We'll have this wine tonight in our room."

The sun skimmed the horizon as their car reached the small El Burgo de Osma hotel. When Miguel changed his single-bed reservation to a double, they smiled reassuringly at one another as the clerk handed over the key. The circular mahogany staircase they climbed to their second-floor room had a worn rug with a large red floral design. A massive, gaudy, crystal chandelier hung from the low ceiling, close enough to touch as they passed by. The hallway walls were painted a glaring turquoise-blue. A dusty, English-style writing desk was the lone piece of furniture outside their room. The bathroom had ugly, ruby-red wall tiles and a garish blue tub. Miguel and Leah's home that night wasn't fancy, only clean, and badly decorated – one step up from a brothel. The rumbling sound of passing trucks piled with harvested grapes filled the room when Miguel opened the window shutters.

They'd planned a walk through town after checking in but Leah knew that wouldn't happen when Miguel led her to the bed with the flat pillows and the crooked three-light sconce above their heads. Endearing words weren't necessary to entice them to undress. His erotic embrace and their combined scents triggered her hand to fondle and place his erection inside of her. Their eyes met lovingly in the dimly lit room as her hips rose to transport him to the purest place within a woman's body, the one she saves for the right lover.

"If I was thirty-two and you also younger, I'd choose you to have my child," he said with his arms straightened over her shoulders and his head bent close to hers. "We could have had a family together. That's how I feel about you, Leah," he added as they moved in moist unison.

She knew sentiments like his often singed a woman's heart. Why would he express such deep wishes if he didn't mean it? Spain and their romance had created explosive and confusing questions for her lonely heart. She believed he carried loneliness too, akin to that of an unfulfilled man grown weary with the hunt for the right woman. If only they'd met earlier in their lives. If only.

"You're Rubenesque. You should be painted," he said and stroked her body when their lovemaking subsided. "Do you know what that means?"

"Of course. Rubens painted rounded women. I'm not their size, but I get your gist. I'd rather have a tummy tuck than a portrait," she said and poked him. She wasn't insulted. Instead, she gracefully accepted his compliment honoring the classical image of Rubenesque women loved by men throughout time.

About 5,000 people lived in sleepy El Burgo de Osma, a pinpoint on Spain's map. Those strolling its narrow streets alongside Miguel and Leah were mostly third-age elders – the label given to seniors in Spain. They dressed in drab green, gray or brown woolens. Many women had high-pitched voices and short-cropped hair that encircled their heads like a bonnet. Their men walked beside them, some carrying canes and wearing berets. The couples were out for their *paseo*. This public display during early evening before dinner has been a ritual for centuries throughout Spain. It began in a Spaniard's childhood; progressed through the teenage years; then continued with young couples pushing baby carriages and finally settled in with later generations, all devotees of the *la familia* concept. Neither Miguel nor Leah had experienced a lasting family life, having short-circuited the process with their divorces.

Leah spoke very little and wasn't at peace when they started their *paseo* after dinner. They mimicked the elders with linked arms and a measured pace, stopping to sightsee along their walk. Both had seen small Spanish towns before but El Burgo de Osma was the smallest they'd seen together. Miguel stopped often to admire the elegant Baroque buildings, cold to the touch, and where he'd run his hand over the discolored and silent walls.

"Imagine the centuries of life this building has witnessed," he said at one stop.

He recalled history so often, along with characters he'd read about in novels, it sounded to Leah as if he couldn't create a life of his own. Was his real life that stymied?

He'd mentioned Susan in random conversations throughout their journey. She was the invisible third person, riding along in the back seat as Miguel sang to Leah and reached for her hand.

"Susan is a good woman. Everyone loves her heart. I can't fault her. I'm the one who's bored stiff. I'll destroy her if I leave the relationship just because of that."

"Life's too short for that screwed-up analysis, Miguel. Don't give in so easily."

"I honestly don't know what to do." Then he added rather abruptly, "Don't get married, Leah. You don't need it." The comment implied Susan was pressing for marriage, a commitment Miguel didn't want.

"I like my single life."

Obviously, she'd achieved most of what she wanted in life. If a second husband were her goal, she'd have one. Miguel told her she didn't appear to be on the prowl but thought she'd bite if someone came along. Unfortunately, being with him signaled she was indeed ready for a steady lover-companion or companion-lover. Was Miguel the true love she longed for? Could they love deeply and honestly resulting in a freedom to keep them together forever?

"This is so weird to talk about living with Susan and stand here with you," he gasped. They'd stopped on a small bridge and he babbled on about his girlfriend while the water babbled below. "I'm sorry, Leah."

"Let's get out of here," she suggested. She didn't acknowledge his apology. Instead, she moved from his side and led them away from the bridge. He'd have to cross another kind of bridge and leave Susan behind if he wanted to be a complete *I* for his future. The bridge became metaphoric for her, too. Had she gone too far on her path as a free woman? What had she done to herself by running away and sleeping with this stranger? Here she was standing on a bridge in El Burgo de Osma, hundreds of miles away from Madrid, and feeling like a jerk. Their run-away trip was supposed to be fun. It wasn't any more.

The third-age elders had vanished when Miguel and Leah retraced their steps through the tiny streets. She found herself peeking through lace curtains into homes where couples sat in their living rooms watching television, sipping from teacups. She liked their permanency.

The silence grew deafening between Miguel and Leah when they entered their garish hotel room. Her mind envisioned a bus ride back to Madrid, alone, after their breakfast. She'd forsake their drive to Siguenza the next day and instead choose a journey back to herself. They needed to part. She didn't want him living with another woman, even if he did want Leah to have his child.

"Good night, Leah," Miguel said as he reached above their heads to shut off the lit wall sconce. "It was a beautiful day traveling with you. I meant everything I said, even the part about having my child." He then curled himself into her body and pulled her close, murmuring that she was a wonderful woman.

Within minutes, they were asleep and never left one another's arms during the night.

After breakfast, Leah said nothing about going back to Madrid. Instead, she returned to her side of the car, kissed Miguel's cheek, buckled up, opened the map and traced the route to Siguenza. The medieval town was once home to chivalrous men defending their fair maidens, debauchery, howling winter nights and romantic siestas. It was their kind of place.

Leah also thought they traveled well together considering they were practically strangers. Could the majority of seatmates run away as lovers? Traveling in a small car was confining but it allowed her to kiss his check whenever she chose. Sharing a hotel room and bathroom were intimate experiences, but they did both with ease. Making love the way they did took some couples years to perfect, but they reached nirvana on the first night. Leah and Miguel acted as if they'd known one another for a lifetime. But she never stopped asking herself: *What's going on here?* She didn't know Miguel's thoughts and chose not to ask him. Why risk a cavalier answer?

Both were quick-witted and a lot of laughter filled the rental car as they rode along. They kept laughing at dinner and often in bed. Their pace had evolved to being surprisingly alike. No one lagged in the morning, although Leah preferred silence for about an hour after rising.

"You talk too much," she once said to him at breakfast.

He stopped mid-sentence and thought about her remark. "I rarely say more than two sentences at home. Actually, nothing in paragraphs any more, but I do talk a lot with you."

"I noticed."

Beautiful vistas can leave an imprint on the traveler's mind. The one etched for her dreams about Miguel materialized during a drive en route to Siguenza. The rolling green hills, terra-cotta earth, purple vineyards and puffy clouds created an idyllic setting for the perfect couple, which they personified in that encapsulated moment.

"Listen to this song. It's about us," she said feeling like a schoolgirl as she pushed the *Don Juan de Marco* soundtrack into the dashboard CD player. She had packed the disk in New York, along with others to keep her company while she stayed alone in her Madrid apartment. She wondered why she'd taken that one CD along for the two-day journey with Miguel. Her favorite lyrics told the story of when a man loves a woman he sees his unborn child in her eyes. Those were the words Miguel whispered to her the night before. When the song ended, Leah stared at the open road.

"Look," Miguel finally said and outstretched his arm. It was covered with goose bumps. "That song chilled me to my bones."

Their home that night was the extraordinary Parador de Siguenza in the town of Siguenza. Built as a castle in the fifth century, by the twelfth century it housed a bishop. Now as Leah and Miguel drove up the winding streets and under a stone arch, the edifice was a government-run and renowned parador overlooking the red tile roofs of the town below. After checking in, Miguel took Leah's hand to walk through the enormous public rooms with vaulted stone ceilings and vintage portraits. He studied the plaques honoring the former medieval occupants and explained their lineage. He led her through the massive, carved wooden doors that opened onto a stone courtyard. In its middle, a gurgling fountain spouted water from a cherub's mouth. Leah had stayed in many paradores, but she'd never been with anyone like Miguel who expressed such enthusiasm. It was close to lunchtime and instead of walking into town, they continued the delightful parador experience in the dining room with suits of armor displayed nearby on red, velvet-covered bases.

"All the food is local," Leah said. "My favorite is *migas*. It's breadcrumbs with a gourmet Spanish twist. The goat is good, too. For dessert, let's split the *Flores de Cabanillas*. It's a pastry shaped like a flower. How's that for telling you what to eat?" she said and looked at him over her menu. He accepted all of her suggestions.

As they dined and admired the surrounding hills and pastureland outside the windows, Miguel revisited his relationship with Susan. They weren't on the same intellectual level. Conversations were a challenge. "People don't always turn out the way you think they are," he sighed. He loved Susan but trying to envision a long life together seemed impossible. They had just moved in together. How could he ask her to leave so quickly?

"You're middle-aged and should be living the life that suits you. What you're doing isn't fair. Set her free. She won't go on her own, I'm sure of that." Leah then filled his glass with wine recommended by the winery owner. "Let me tell you a story about a friend who continued a marriage year after year after year until she couldn't take it anymore."

"Please do," he said and leaned back in his chair.

Leah was a natural-born storyteller and Miguel was a captive lunch partner that day, and so she began sharing her friend Nellie's remarkable tale. It was steeped in broken hearts and lost chances with a remarkable happy conclusion. Leah hoped Miguel would grasp the story's meaning that life shouldn't be lived with self-inflicted wounds. Slowly and carefully choosing her words, she revealed Nellie's courageous and life-altering decision.

"I'll start with the shocking end and back into this one," Leah said to get his immediate attention.

At age fifty-two and after twenty-five years of marriage, Nellie packed a suitcase and drove away from home, never to return to her unsuspecting husband and three teenage children leading their normal lives in the upstairs living room. She left them for Brian, a former lover, with whom she had had a yearlong affair early in her marriage. When her husband discovered the affair, a horrific fight ensured, with fists flying between the men. Horrified and scared, Nellie remained in her empty marriage but always mourning the loss of Brian's true love. He thought of her daily and also stayed in his loveless marriage.

Twenty-three years later, Brian called Nellie after his wife died. Could they meet just to say hello? She agreed, wanting the reunion to create a new reality to destroy her daydreams. Instead, their love returned in waves. She could never leave Brian again nor could she battle out a divorce with her husband. Instead, she drove away from her marital home and gave up the designer kitchen, the parties, the full wardrobe and the empty marriage for her true destiny. Nellie eventually got her divorce. She and Brian went on to marry, as did her ex-husband.

"So what do you think of Nellie's story, Miguel? Do you agree a person shouldn't be in an intimate relationship and want to be with someone else?"

"Great story, Leah. Can't you just see the jilted husband looking all over the house for his wife? Jesus, what a scenario."

She dropped the subject.

~ ♡ ~

Whenever Miguel and Leah checked into a new hotel, she assumed they'd wait until nightfall to continue their beautiful lovemaking. But that didn't happen in Siguenza either. As the sliver of dusk's light streamed through their bedroom windows, they were making love.

"There, I said it," he whispered.

"What did you say?"

"I love you, Leah."

"And I love you, too."

Was she insane to say that to him? How could they be in love? Impossible, but it sounded good. She hadn't heard a man say those three tender words in a long time. Her children and dear friends said them to her. But her familial life hadn't replaced the need for a man-woman love. And why did Miguel say it when he had a girlfriend at home? Something was deeply wrong in Virginia.

"You wouldn't try to domesticate me?" he asked cuddling up alongside of her.

"No reason to do that."

Leah knew she was a city girl with no interest in a manicured lawn or canning blueberries. She'd lived alone for so many years she now treasured her freedom to the point of isolation. If Miguel and she continued beyond Spain, she'd suggest they live apart; he in Virginia, and she in New York.

Miguel was uncharacteristically quiet when they dressed. Too quiet. "Leah, I'm sorry, but I have to call Susan from this room. I don't travel with a cell phone. Several days have passed without any contact from me. I'm so sorry, but she'll go berserk wondering if I'm okay." He looked defeated.

"I'm a big girl. I understand. I'll meet you in the lobby."

Leah left the room, walked through the lobby, the heavy wooden front doors and down a hilly street. She walked into the first bar she spotted. It was filled with noisy patrons who were sipping drinks and littering the floor with olive pits and peanut shells. Several teenagers jostled one another at an arcade game with multi-colored lights and repetitive bells. A soccer game blared from the overhead TV, but Leah was numb to noise.

"*Una cerveza, por favor,*" she said to the bartender.

Sipping beer, she adjusted to the din and thought about her startling journey with Miguel. He was a terrific communicator. He was a fantastic lover. But they weren't a real couple outside of Spain. Maybe he needed their memory to keep going at home. She didn't. Being with him catapulted her back to the classic push-pull contradiction she'd struggled with for years. She adored the sex but not the day-to-day life with a man. She couldn't commit either. Her obsession with an independent life had produced a woman with a Ph.D. in exit strategy. But Miguel wasn't engaged or married to Susan. He was quasi-single. Maybe he'd leave Susan, after all. Maybe, maybe, maybe.

One hour and another beer later, she remembered telling Miguel she'd meet him in the parador lobby. She paid the check and left the bar. The familiar deafening silence of night in many darkened Spanish towns surrounded her as she traced her footsteps back to the parador. She was calm, distracted only by the occasional cat that darted past headed for an obscure alley. She'd bolted on Miguel. Did he stay in their room or was he walking alone in Siguenza? As she trudged up the last hill, she decided to return to Madrid the next day. She had to get away from his abduction of her heart.

"Where are you? Are you okay? I'm worried about you," Miguel said when Leah's cell phone rang in the parador's parking lot. "Look up. I'm in the window."

She saw him waving from their bedroom like a fair maiden welcoming her lover home, except the roles were reversed. When she returned to their room, there was a gift waiting for Leah. Miguel had purchased a lovely necklace in Segovia. It was the perfect choice, as if he'd chosen her gifts for a lifetime. He slipped it over her neck just before they walked down hilly Siguenza, ending up at a pizza parlor. Susan wasn't home so he left a message. Leah swallowed the lump in her throat when she heard his girlfriend's name. She didn't mention her decision to return to Madrid in the morning. Why sabotage a wonderful night of lovemaking?

Leah's soul-searching long walk and deep talk did little good for her resolve to return to Madrid. The next morning she and Miguel drove down the parador's driveway headed for Cuenca and another unknown. She was again thrilled to be at his side. He was an informed guidebook traveler. That pleased her since he narrated their trip with historical facts and lively anecdotes. She was more of an intuitive traveler, one who arrived with fresh eyes and a blank notebook in which she'd record her surroundings, pointing out oddities Miguel missed.

"Have you ever driven in Spain on your own?" he asked along their ride. "Most women wouldn't do that, but I suspect you have."

"Yes, I have. Years ago when I was on a writing assignment about Spanish products, I drove throughout the country and into the lesser-known regions of Spain."

One day she'd be at a Valencia factory where local women hand-painted whimsical scenes on cloth fans. The next day she'd tour a guitar factory where the workers tested the instruments. Aromas from a candy factory teeming with roasted almonds and honey clung to her clothing. At wine bodegas, she'd sip from a communal cup and tour the deep caves that housed the vintage. A herd of goats might walk past an opened door, signaling their arrival with the clanging of their neck bells. Many times a horse-drawn cart brimming with fruit slowed her car. The driver and Leah headed toward a deep-red sunset where its color matched the vineyards on both sides of the road.

"What a life," Miguel said. "You really do know this country. You love it, too. I can hear it in your voice."

"It's cemented in my soul. I can't explain how a woman from New England had her heart, imagination and soul captured so readily. Was it a past life?" she asked with a glint in her eye. "But I made a stupid mistake once when driving alone into the dark night. Want to hear the long story?" she asked him.

"Obviously, yes. We've got time before we reach Cuenca. I love your storytelling. Begin."

The terrifying incident happened one pitch-black, rainy night in southern Spain on her way to a remote parador. The day's journey had taken her from a large city to smaller towns to tiny villages to long stretches of uninhabited land. With nightfall approaching, she worried that her reservation would be canceled or no rooms would be available if she arrived late.

Miles of black trees passed by her small car with only an occasional moonbeam flickering through the darkness like a distant beacon. She turned the radio up louder and tapped out a Spanish tune on the steering wheel to keep herself focused and calm. Finally, a signpost indicated a town several kilometers ahead. Within minutes, she parked in front of a small store and entered. Several men stood at the bar beside the cash register and eyed Leah suspiciously. Thankfully, the payphone worked and she confirmed the parador reservation. The men listened as she stumbled through the call speaking Spanish and English. One man stared at her more than the others.

When she returned to her car, she locked the doors, turned on the ignition and sped away into unfamiliar terrain. A drizzle began. Within minutes, a steady rain pelted the car, enough for her to increase the wipers' speed and squint through the windshield. An approaching road sign showed the parador's logo and thirty kilometers to go, approximately the same amount of minutes on the dark road through heavy rain. Fatigue and loneliness took hold.

The rear-view mirror revealed another car gaining speed

steadily until it slowed when it reached her car. Its headlights flickered. The horn blew, fast and repeatedly. What had she done? Was it the police? Should she stop? Yes. Something must be wrong with her car. She pulled over and rolled down her window. Splashes of cool, wet rain dripped on her arm. The car behind her pulled over with its headlights on high beam. Their windshield wipers clicked in unison. A man got out and approached Leah's side of the car. She sensed danger. Terror filled her chest. Her knees knocked together, then shook beyond her control. It was a strange reflex to have muscles contract from fear.

The man raised his flashlight's beam into her face. She squinted. He said something in Spanish. Within seconds, his other hand grabbed Leah's breast as he tried to pull her closer to the door. She was terrified far beyond a level she'd ever known as she struggled against his force. Rape. Sodomy. Strangulation. A savage beating. Left by the roadside. Visions of brutality at the hands of a lunatic on a lonely Spanish road flashed before her eyes as the attacker dropped the flashlight and put his other hand into the car.

She screamed a primal, earthy, shriek into the darkness. He clutched at her breast even harder. Her hands shook uncontrollably, but she somehow found a steadiness to put her left hand on the window handle. Swiftly and with no concern for her attacker's arm, she rolled it up until it crunched his wiggling hand against the top of the doorframe. He screamed into the darkness. He banged his other hand hard against the window. She continued to squeeze his hand with the window and then rolled it down just enough so he could wrench it out from the narrow slot before she rolled it back up.

"I can't drive with you telling me this awful story. I'm

pulling over. What happened next?" Miguel asked, staring intently at Leah.

"Mercifully, my car had an automatic shift, and it idled smoothly during the attack. With his menacing hand withering in pain outside the window, I floored the accelerator and sped into the darkness. My heart was pounding like a tribal war drum."

"Jesus. And you're alive to tell this. You're quite a woman. I knew it. You've got balls."

She continued on. The attacker's car followed her for several kilometers. One wrong turn, one swerve on a soft shoulder and she'd tumble down thousands of feet, stripping bark off trees, left to die a slow, lonely, painful death in some ravine. Never in her life had she prayed for safety as much as she did that night. Eventually, her attacker's car slowed and disappeared from her rear-view mirror. Still shaking from fear, she continued on until the blackened macadam turned into a dirt road and then into the parador's driveway.

Inside the former castle, a magnificent antique suit of armor, complete with spear, guarded the entrance. Large, wrought-iron lanterns hung from wood-hewn rafters and stenciled wood decorated the reception desk. Sprays of dried grains and flowers stood majestically from terra-cotta planters lining the lobby. Slowly, she began to recover a very fragile sense of security. Outside her bedroom window, a wolf howled furtively and jolted her awake several times.

"I hugged myself for long periods that night knowing I'd learned an invaluable lesson about traveling alone and stopping in the middle of a dark road. I hated men, too," she told Miguel.

Cuenca was packed with holiday-weekend visitors when they arrived. Miguel changed another single-bed hotel room to a double at their newest hideaway. With the small city awaiting them, they walked hand-in-hand through the hotel doorway to climb steep walkways and peer over walls into deep valleys. Their lighthearted mood buoyed their steps. Here and there they'd sneak a quick kiss or two in a doorway, oblivious to people nearby. At the tiny square in front of Basílica de Nuestra Señora de Gracia with cars honking beside them, they stopped at an outdoor café to nibble on *Jamon Serrano*, *Manchego* cheese and sip beers.

"So what are your plans when you get back to New York?" Miguel asked.

Leah wondered whether to mention Dana's accelerated wedding plans and not wanting to attend the wedding alone. The desire to reveal more of her personal life nagged at her in Spain, often in quiet moments as they drove along. She hadn't completely tackled the heavy topic because their trip was lighthearted.

"I've glossed over major facts about my Rhode Island background. They didn't seem relevant when we first met, but I want to tell you now. Perhaps they'll help you understand what I'm facing when I leave Spain. I call that person from Rhode Island *my former self*. She's a woman I don't recognize anymore. But I have to face her again."

"I'm all ears. I'm also your friend so don't hold back. I want to know everything. You're the only person who can tell your story," he said and pulled his chair closer to hold her hand.

"My ex-husband, Jim McCord, was my first love and the father of my two children. But as our years dragged on, I realized we had married too young. Despite loving motherhood, I grew disenchanted with marriage and the lack of communication with him. When financial problems grew and we stagnated as a couple, I broke away to expand my mind by enrolling in a creative writing class. It captivated me, enough to inspire a career. But Jim and I fought endlessly over my growth. He wanted his wife at home. I wanted out. His oppression unwittingly set me free and on the path to where I am now."

"Obviously," Miguel said. "You're still at that path."

"It wasn't that easy," she said. "However, our children were practically grown when we divorced. So I told Jim I'd leave the house. In fact, I left all the furniture, drapes, kitchen stuff, beds…you name it. I moved to New York. It was only fair I leave with nothing but me. He was the better parent and needed a complete home to make the divorce work. At that point, we didn't have an ounce of fight left. We both needed to move on, even though one of us was his beloved wife."

She wasn't a stupid woman Leah told Miguel. To leverage a divorce that could devastate her relationship with her children, bankrupt her financially, banish her socially and eventually cause a lifetime of regret was a heart-stopping choice to make in her early forties. But to improve the quality of her children's lives, she'd have to improve the quality of hers. She'd risk the unknown, all alone. She remembered when Rhode Island's landscape with its mile-long beaches, small towns and industrial complexes slowly vanished as the plane lifted into the clouds. Fear of the unknown overcame her as the humbling and terrifying adventure was about to begin. As Leah chronicled her path out of Rhode Island that resulted in her sitting in Cuenca with Miguel, he kept nodding his head in approval.

"I knew I liked you when we met. Now I love you even more after that incredible story. Congratulations on a brave life well-lived to date," he said.

"May I add that as the years passed my splintered family remained intact as strong individuals," she said. "It wasn't all about me. I would have returned to Rhode Island in a heartbeat if they weren't doing well. The children received excellent educations and prospered. Jim married Sun-Hee Wong after meeting her at choir practice. She was a recent arrival in Rhode Island and 25 years his junior. Nine months later, baby Max arrived."

"He married a younger woman and had a child? Why?" Miguel asked incredulously.

"Don't know. Not my choice and not my kid, but Jim always wanted a woman at home with children in tow. Now he's got another one."

"You made the right decision to go it alone. Divorcing is a hellish process. Many people wait too long, or never live the life they should," Miguel said. "I admire your courage."

Leah went on to tell him that Dana followed her mother's lead and moved to New York for a nursing career. She was engaged to Steve Dunlop, a pediatrician, and they wanted a traditional wedding in Rhode Island. "My daughter and Steve will pay for some of the wedding but hope Jim and I will chip in. I'm not sure how to handle the finances with my ex-husband," Leah said. "But that's not my biggest problem. Showing up alone bothers me most."

She'd be as much a focal point as her beautiful daughter. Hometown people were curious about Leah. Living alone translated to failure in most people's eyes. Dana's wedding day introduced a level of anxiety she hadn't experienced before about being single. The whole dilemma bothered her.

"Don't you have a friend to accompany you?" Miguel asked.

"I don't want that. I want someone special."

"Oh, don't worry about it too much. It's just a day."

"What are you talking about? It's an *important* day to me." Then she leaned forward in her chair and rested her hand on Miguel's knee. She looked him straight in the eye and hoped he knew what was coming. "Why don't you take me to my daughter's wedding? You're that special now."

He stiffened in his seat. His eyes left hers and scanned a nearby table. He bit his lower lip and sighed deeply. "We both know the facts about when I return to Virginia. What you're asking is not realistic."

"Yeah. That's right. We're only temporary. Guess I forgot."

It shocked her to realize how devastated she felt when he refused. But, of course, he had to. He lived with Susan, the imaginary third person tagging along that afternoon. But Leah was in love with Miguel. She'd known it since their first night in Segovia, but she stifled that truth. She knew it when she was the first to awake and followed the outline of his chiseled face beside her. She listened to every word he spoke to her each day as they covered a kaleidoscope of subjects. There she sat at an outdoor café with the man of her dreams – and he lived with another woman. With nothing left to say or ask at that empty moment, she changed the awkward subject.

"So what are your plans when you return to Virginia?" she asked casually.

"I've got clients to see. Bills to pay. Susan and I will host a large party to celebrate our new home."

"A party? You're sitting with me in Cuenca having shared a few beds along the way and Susan is home planning to celebrate the two of you living together? Cancel it." Leah shook her head in amazement. Foolishly and in a delusional state of mind, she thought of Susan as the other woman.

"I can't. The wine's been bought."

"How can you be involved with her and do what you've done with me? How, Miguel? Explain it," she demanded in disgust. He was a committed man who had asked Susan to move in with him. How could he sleep beside her and profess his love for Leah? She was baffled and angry, more with herself than with him.

"I have no guilt being here with you. I now know what I am. This is not an affair. It's a love story. You should write about it," he said sheepishly.

"Jesus Christ," she swore, loud enough for a passerby to glance her way. "Write about it? What are the opening and closing lines? Is it fiction or not?"

He didn't answer her outburst. She avoided his eyes and watched the crowd pass until she pushed back on her metal slotted chair beside the rickety café table. When Leah reached for her handbag ready to leave their table, Miguel got up, too, but his chair caught on the edge of the cobblestone sidewalk and toppled over.

"This isn't for me, Miguel. I'm done with affairs. It's my former life," she said.

"I don't know what to do. What can I do? I need time to think," he said and righted the chair.

"The plane ride, Segovia, El Burgo de Osma, Siguenza and now Cuenca are too much to accept as a fly-by-night dalliance. This affair is escalating," she told him. "Love stories are supposed to have a happy ending. Will ours?"

He nodded an understanding and reached for her hand, motioning with his head to walk along a narrow pathway beside the church. Despite holding hands, they walked in silence. It was awkward now. Leah's reality had turned ugly but they continued their Cuenca visit. At dusk and still with a strain between them, they ended their touristic day in a former home attached to the side of a cliff transformed into the Museo de Arte Abstracto Español.

Their quiet and tidy hotel room that night didn't compare to the impressive parador where Miguel had professed his love for Leah.

"This is our sixth time making love. You're in my heart, Leah," he said tenderly on their bed. "I'm falling deeper in love with you. I don't know what to do. It wasn't supposed to be this way. I'm frightened to leave you; frightened to think about knowing you in the States and frightened you'll leave me," he whispered in her ear.

Leah only nodded her head, signaling she understood. She knew his heart. It matched hers precisely.

During breakfast that day, they had discussed his two remaining nights in Spain. One would be spent with her in Cuenca. She'd definitely return to Madrid the next morning. For his last night, he needed solitude to prepare for his return to Virginia. Their final goodbye would be by phone. He'd probably be at the airport. She'd be in her Madrid apartment.

After their morning shower together, she took the tiny hotel soap, as she'd done from all their hotels. For showers at home, she'd rub it over her body to simulate his touch. Her eyes made one last sweep of their room to ensure nothing remained except her broken heart lying on the rumpled sheets.

Oh how she wanted to dissolve into tears when she thought about leaving him after breakfast. Instead, she watched as he sat on their bed, flipping through his guidebook with his magnificent fingers tracing the route from Cuenca to El Toboso.

"Here's where we're going today," he said and pointed to the Museo Casa Natal de Cervantes in the center of the small town. "Can you imagine being in La Mancha? Land of Don Quixote. I'll be him today. You can be Dulcinea. Ready?" he gushed.

"El Toboso with you? What day together? I'm taking a train back to Madrid. Don't you remember? You're traveling alone from now on," she said in exasperation.

"Don't go yet. I'll miss you. We're buddies on the road," he said with pleading eyes.

"One more day together and that's it, Miguel. When we reach Alcalá de Henares tonight, I'm going to Madrid. You're sleeping alone."

~ ♡ ~

Miguel and Leah reached tiny El Toboso at lunchtime. He chose a restaurant located in an alleyway with canaries chirping in overhead cages. They were led to a back table where it was unusually quiet by Spanish standards. After their waiter left their table, Leah's eyes avoided Miguel's. Instead, they fixated on the wine glass in her hand as she swirled its contents.

"You've left me, Leah. I can feel it. What are you contemplating?" he asked.

"Something's wrong with your center and how it reacts to women. Forgive me, please, but have you considered seeing a shrink?"

"I saw one already. He helped me identify that I fall deeply in love immediately and fall out of it usually within three months. We were working on a solution, but I stopped going."

"This is a character flaw, Miguel. You're hurting women, deeply."

"I fight the falling-out-of-love part. I tell myself it happens to everyone, but why me and why so soon? So I stay in a relationship, faking it most of the time and wanting to be alone. But I also need a woman in my life. I'm not a monk. Most women want a committed relationship, and I comply. I can't say I blame them."

"Well, at least you're aware. Falling out of lust or love doesn't happen to everyone or every man. Cheap excuse. There's an immaturity here with you. You're knocking on the door of sixty. It might be time to man-up and go back into therapy. Try a woman psychologist this time and ask her to explain a woman's heart."

"I hear you. But I am myself and my circumstances," he said, repeating Spanish philosopher, José Ortega y Gasset's quote. "I suffer, too, with my dishonest behavior. But I repeat and repeat and repeat my erratic approach with women. I'm looking for answers and trying to change."

"When I remove this destructive behavior and make my way to that loving heart of yours, I accept you for now. There's no one like you for me. Thank you for graciously accepting my suggestion to seek help," Leah said.

To ward off the three-course lunch's sleepy aftermath, they decided to visit Belmonte Castle, which was a drive of 30 kilometres away. The fifteenth-century Gothic structure was built in the form of a six-pointed star with a cylindrical tower at the end of each. Leah and Miguel climbed a winding, dank staircase that opened at the castle's top. A gentle wind blew over their bodies, which were rarely more than a few inches apart, their hands even closer. Below were long expanses of parched valleys, a small village and the ever-present church spire in the distance.

With sunset nearing, they returned to El Toboso to visit the Cervantes' museum where Miguel lingered at the exhibits. Back in their car, the region's romantic windmills diminished in their rear-view mirror as they headed for Alcalá de Henares, Cervantes' birthplace, several hours away toward Madrid.

Leah sensed that Miguel's return to Virginia the next day weighed heavily on his mind. It paralyzed hers. The tension in the car was palpable.

"I don't want to go home," he finally said.

"Change your life, Miguel," she blurted out. "Live in Spain if you want to return to your roots. Find work you can do in both countries. You're single. There's no family life to disrupt. It's possible to change one's life. I did it and never looked back."

"Me pongo triste," he said and wiped at a tear. "You're deep inside me, Leah. I haven't cried like this in a long time. I don't know what to do. Meeting you unearthed a rush of buried emotional roots. I can't digest it all except to know that I love you deeply. It can't be possible in such a short time."

"Follow your heart. Don't be so hard on yourself. Stop thinking about us; concentrate on where you want to be." Leah struggled trying not to cry with him.

"I'm having *agita* right now," she said in the moonlight. They had reached their destination but were driving around aimlessly looking for the hotel. She hated where she was. She hated herself. She hated him. A train to Madrid seemed unlikely. If they couldn't find their hotel, how could they find the train station?

"It's too late for you to return to Madrid. Stay with me tonight," he said.

"Not the plan but what else can I do? Find a taxi driver and ask for directions to the hotel. We're going in circles now."

It aggravated her when Miguel carried on a lengthy conversation in Spanish with the hotel clerk. Once in their room, she dallied and sent text messages to friends. When he hung up her jacket, she placed it back on her suitcase when he showered. She was hungry and he wasn't so she left him and went to a nearby cafe, grateful to dine alone. He called her cell phone for directions to the restaurant and joined her, an angry man deep in thought. Whatever they discussed produced a sulk from him or from her.

After dinner, they sat in the hotel's small lounge, the only patrons. He sipped a scotch and grew angrier, picking apart subjects Leah presented. Something had turned him into a different man than the one she'd traveled with. Rather than have an angry dialogue, she placated him until they were in their room again and lay together for the last time.

"How can I leave my brothers and the family business?" he asked her and propped himself up on his pillows. There was fury in his eyes. "How can I leave everything behind and move back to Spain? What about Susan and our furniture?" Scenarios about leaving Spain as a child spewed out. His voice grew louder. His body stiffened with anger.

"I was only making a suggestion to change your life. That's all. Do what you want," Leah said. She hadn't seen this behavior before. For a split second, she was frightened enough to want her own room. Her mind enacted a scenario where she jumped out of bed, dressed quickly, grabbed her purse, ran to the hallway hoping an elevator arrived quickly to take her to the lobby's reservation desk.

"You frighten me," she said, cowering nude beside him. "Look at the good side of life. You're a successful executive. People love you. You have self-worth. Give up this anger,

Miguel," she pleaded and inched herself up on one elbow to face him.

He ignored her and stared straight ahead. He took breaths deep enough for his shoulders to lift and recede into his propped pillows.

"You should have returned to Madrid this morning," he said not looking at her. "I didn't want you to see this side of me. It's a dark moment. I feel trapped in this room knowing I'll wake up and leave Spain tomorrow, which means leaving you. Leaving you means I face my day-to-day life with Susan. If she asks me for details about my trip, what do I say? When we look at the photos – some you took of me – how will I react? I'm a monogamous man. I never did this cheating life before, and I never will again."

"I don't have a clue how you'll handle this. I'm glad I'm not you."

"Good night, Leah. I can't discuss this with you anymore," he said and lowered the pillows under his head.

"Good night, Miguel. And be nice to me because I'm carrying your baby," she kidded as she returned his kiss with several small ones.

He then rolled on top of her, kissed her intently, entered her and climaxed in five minutes. Leah was emotionally absent. Who was this different man?

While he slept, she assessed their last night as the traffic screeched below the room. Perhaps his imminent return home and the inner self he struggled with on a daily basis caused the bizarre behavior. Spain, its history, the ancient buildings, his native language, his freedom and Leah were slipping away. These important losses defined who he was – the real Miguel, not the man in Virginia.

At the break of dawn, they checked out of their last hotel, found a small restaurant and shared hot chocolate and *churros* alongside many sleep-eyed patrons beginning or ending their day.

"I'm deeply sorry for my behavior last night. No excuses for it. I go there sometimes. That's how I acted with my ex-wife. That's why I divorced her. It's painful behavior for those around me when I'm feeling trapped with no way out," Miguel said lowering his eyes.

"You're forgiven. I'd say I won't accept it in the future, but there's no future for us."

After his last sip of hot chocolate, Miguel dabbed at his mouth with a skimpy paper napkin, crumbled it and dropped it on the floor, which was customary in Spain. He looked at Leah's face and pulled a digital camera from his coat pocket. He leaned back in his chair and focused the lens on her half-smile and questioning eyes.

It was the fifth day of her two-day wardrobe. She hoped the wrinkles didn't show. He pressed the shutter. Pleased with her image on the LCD screen, he smiled and returned the camera to his pocket.

Their last drive together was a sad one. No more little towns for them. No more moonlight outside their windows as they made love. They were en route to Madrid's Barajas Airport, an hour's ride away.

"How about we meet in Spain again? We travel well together," he said.

"How about you first come to New York to visit me?"

"How about I give you my personal office telephone number?"

"I'll never call so don't bother. I broke a pact with myself.

85

The next man I made love to would begin a serious relationship. I deceived myself by being with you. I don't want a double life."

"What we shared isn't a double life. We were one very special couple here in Spain. Don't be so hard on yourself."

"I don't want to betray women. That's what I did to Susan."

"So did I," he said quickly.

"Oh well, a few weeks of breaking a new promise isn't that much of a big deal. You were worth the slip up," she said and put her hand on his thigh.

"Leah, my dear, it's a love story. Don't forget that or mess it up with too much examination."

"Do you think I ran away with you as a rebound because of what happened with Javier?"

"No. That affair was over when you met him in Salamanca. I knew he wasn't the man for you. He was perfect for the woman he remembered."

"Are you perfect for me?"

"Don't start that again, please."

"Why do I feel like I deceived myself?"

"You didn't deceive yourself. What happened was authentic. The magic of Spain helped, too. When we return home, let's never forget what happened to us. Promise?"

"Promise."

At the airline check-in counter, Miguel was talkative and animated. Leah was contemplative and still. Her heart hurt as his suitcases disappeared on the beltway. They took her delusions about their relationship as they rolled out of sight. His departure was much tougher to endure than she'd imagined.

"Well, this is it, Leah. What an incredible journey with my charming seatmate," he said when the security checkpoint blocked them from going any farther. He continued their good-bye kiss with one blown from his outstretched hand as she backed away from him.

Their love story continued to consume and sadden Leah as she made her way back to her Madrid apartment. She licked her lips on the subway platform to taste his farewell kiss. A fantasy arose as she saw herself dancing with him at Dana's wedding. But she couldn't put him in the single-guy category. A familiar feeling associated with her man returning to another woman was the reality. She disliked herself at a deep level. But instead of dwelling on pain, she made herself concentrate on the joy they'd experienced. She'd change her approach to men tomorrow. Miguel was her last mistake.

It was lonely when she entered her Madrid home despite the noise that lifted up from the streets. She opened the patio doors and stood on the balcony, staring into a brilliant sun-filled and cloudless sky. It was a perfect day to fly. She imagined Miguel settling into his seat. When she imagined his seatbelt buckling shut, the sound pierced her heart and deeply enough to realize that their love story was finally over.

"How come you're not calling me? Still doing research outside of Madrid?" Rocío said with a smirk when she met Leah for lunch.

It was the day after Miguel's departure and Leah was still in the titillating stage from their whirlwind affair. Should she tell Rocío more about him? Her dear friend appeared jaded when they discussed men, although her mood that day was difficult to pinpoint.

"I lied to you," Leah confessed and avoided Rocío's eyes. "Maria from the tourist office didn't invite me to Seville. I met

Miguel again in Salamanca. We traveled through the Wine Region and into Castilla-La Mancha. He left yesterday for Virginia."

Rocío pursed her lips and shook her head in bewilderment. "Silly woman, Leah. Why did you do that? Now you're hurting. I know you."

"Sure I'm hurting. So what else is new? What do you think, Rocío?" Leah gushed childlike as she skipped over Rocío's disparaging words. "Miguel said I'm an eighteenth-century courtesan. Did he mean I'm a twenty-first-century whore? He said I'm Rubenesque and should be painted. Is that an insult? The next man was supposed to be my last lover," she sighed. "I broke that pact with myself, but Miguel said making love is what adults do. What do you think?"

"Sex is a mystery," Rocío said and scrunched her face. "Whatever he said to you, good or bad, don't take it personally. He's a man."

Leah thought their conversation about men probably made Rocío too contemplative about sex and emotions. But she valued her observations so she added that Miguel cried when they parted. She also revealed their last night together when he became a mean and angry person, someone unknown before.

"He's an emotionally unstable man, Leah. Stay away because he won't leave you alone. There have been many women in his life. He's never content. Always looking for the ideal woman. I haven't slept with him and I can judge more easily than you can. He's a charmer. He's wonderful at falling in love but a disaster staying there. What makes you think you're so different from the other women he's bedded?"

"We're alike. I'm the ultimate collector of affections and always looking, too. Our souls are united at a deep emotional level. But did I ever fall hard in love with him. Should I call him when I get back to New York?"

"No. You'll regret it. How delusional are you? He lives with a woman. He's a creep for moving in with her and the next week traveling around Spain with you."

"He's not a creep. Don't label him. He doesn't want to live with her. It just happened. Convenience, shared expenses, someone to date on Saturday, reasons like that. He's scared to leave because he's left many others. Traveling together as strangers revealed volumes about him and me. I know I'm right about him. He's a good guy, Rocío."

"Yes, he does want to stay with the girlfriend. She's his cover. Easy to lie to. Easy to live with. She'll wait for him to come home from his solo adventures. It's an extremely difficult decision for him to leave her at this stage of his life, maybe too difficult. He doesn't have the most important quality needed for the decision."

"What's that?" Leah asked leaning over her plate, entranced with Rocío's take on Miguel.

"Courage. He's weak. You're not, Leah. You and I know that a new affair, hot lovemaking and scheming to make it all work fails every time. He knows it, too. Stay away from him because he'll find and exploit your weakest point."

"He has courage. I'm sure. We have already discussed his behavior with women. He's aware of it. On the other hand, it takes a lot to search for the right woman. I've been looking for the right guy for years now. I think you and I can agree with that statement. But I don't move in with them. Miguel has taken the search to a whole other level. But thanks for your observations. Let's see how this plays out. I can always put this experience in a novel."

"Now you're talking. That's where it belongs," Rocío said. She paid the check and invited Leah to the Museo del Romanticismo. "In English, it's the Romance Museum but it sounds better in Spanish."

The museum was a few blocks from the restaurant, giving them a chance to window shop and stroll with linked arms. Turning the corner onto Calle San Mateo, they came upon a long line that had formed outside the former small palace sandwiched between two buildings. Its front was painted a deep shade of terra cotta. Inside, two courtyards, a garden and a petite café echoed the theme of Spain's early-nineteenth-century Romantic Movement. Brocade prints and gold taffeta draperies; full-sized paintings of noblemen; glistening chandeliers; a spinet piano; English and French crockery; dollhouses and hand-painted fans created an unforgettable ambiance.

"This is your kind of place," Rocío said softly so as not to disturb the other visitors.

"Some of these things are mine. Didn't you know I was a Spanish *countessa* centuries ago?" Leah said and opened her notebook to write.

CHAPTER FIVE

THE DAY AFTER MIGUEL ARRIVED HOME, he called Leah from his private office phone. It was 6:00 p.m. in Virginia but midnight in Madrid. The call startled her, and she sat up ramrod straight in bed.

"Don't think I forgot you. I miss you a lot," he said as she lay back down and cradled the cell phone against her ear.

His words pierced her Miguel-proof heart, spinning it out of control – again – with the melodic tone of his romantic voice. Rocío had convinced her they'd never be a public couple because he lived with Susan. Leah eventually agreed and relegated their run-away affair to being a delightful fluke.

"I'm half of a whole since you left," she said softly. "How was the flight? And what happened when you got home?"

"Smooth flight all the way. Arriving home was tough," he said sadly. "Susan met me at the airport. I suffered from guilt when she hugged me. She's a good person. I was two people during the ride home – thinking about you, yet pleased to see her. We discussed Spain but I saw you beside me. I've never been two personalities before. It's disgusting. This is so weird. I don't want to hurt her."

"So why call me?" Leah said dejectedly. The vivid memories of their time together evaporated when she heard Susan's name.

"Because I can't help myself. Can we travel again? We love Spain, and I love you. What do you think?"

"I'm not thinking right now. Too many maybes."

"I meant everything I said to you, Leah," were Miguel's parting words after an hour's conversation. She detected a faint kiss transmitted through the crackled international phone line.

She didn't expect a call the next night but missed Miguel's voice, his essence, his everything when her phone was silent. Around midnight, her romantic mind replayed his last call where he said the differences between he and Susan continued to manifest. It was instantly noticeable when he arrived home, making the decision to stay with her a greater challenge. Where he'd once accepted his fate that he'd never find the right woman, meeting Leah left him deeply conflicted.

I love you, Leah. Miguel's vow echoed in her mind. Sitting alone in her apartment, her self-imposed pact not to call a committed man wavered. She stared at the computer screen, hoping to write as a distraction. The rock-solid decision not to call Miguel eventually cracked. Her cell phone rolled in her hand, as she struggled with the decision. Call him or not? Rocío's warning replayed in her head. Miguel was weak. He used charm to lure women like Leah into his arms and then bed. He was wrong for her at this point in her life. She needed a steady, trustworthy companion. Someone to love forever. Someone to take to Dana's wedding. It wasn't Miguel. And remember, he lives with a woman who trusts him when he travels alone.

As the phone twirled in her hand, she tightened her grasp until she finally stopped and looked at the screen. She scrolled to the Received function, saw Miguel's office phone number, bit her lower lip and pressed Call. Anxiety fluttered in her heart with each elongated ring. But despite the anticipation and the sexual moistening she felt as she waited for his voice, the call turned out to be one she should never have made.

"Wow," he gasped. "Hello, Leah. What a surprise. How did you get my private number?"

"It's on my cell phone. You called me. Remember? How are you?"

"I'm hung over. Susan and I toasted my return last night with the wine I purchased in that Segovia restaurant where you and I dined."

Leah hoped he saw her face with his first sip. Although she heard his words, her heart barely withstood the cruelty of what he'd just said. She was still reeling from calling him.

"I'm having a hard time forgetting you, Miguel. You're supposed to be an instant memory, not someone who captured my heart and mind," she confessed. "It's wonderful to hear your voice again."

"Nice to hear you, too. Are you calling to invite me to New York when you get home?"

Leah couldn't decipher whether his tone was sarcastic or playful. "Maybe. If you create a new life for yourself, then maybe, and it's a huge maybe, we could plan a trip or you'd simply visit me in New York."

"I'm happy to be home, happy to be with Susan and happy to sleep with her again. Meeting you in New York is too deceitful and risky," he said with a chill in his voice, adding that the nationwide real estate market had plunged. He'd lose a significant sum if he walked away from his recent home purchase. "I can't say I'll spend the rest of my life with her, but

I'm not thinking about leaving right now."

Who is this man on the phone talking to me? Leah was stunned. This heartless person couldn't be Miguel. It wasn't the sweet, loving man who'd called the night before. Was he that strange, angry man she knew in Alcalá de Henares during their awful last night? She kept the conversation light to deflect his devastating words. Eventually, they talked about her last week alone in Madrid and their time together in Spain.

"I love you, Leah," he said sweetly. "Everything I said to you in Spain was true. I can't continue with you in the States. It's cruel to Susan, to you and it turns me into a deceiving liar, yet again. We'll just have to cherish the memories we created."

After they ended the call, Leah was physically numb and emotionally demolished. What to do? What to think? How to feel after a devastating conversation with the man of her dreams who'd brushed her off like an annoying fly. Or was he really a nightmare of a man? A monster lover? What was going on? How quickly his temperament changed once Leah hovered over his home base. She disgusted herself at a deep level. Here she was a grown woman going through a teenager drama over a boyfriend. But he wasn't her boyfriend. She'd only known him for two weeks. He was Susan's boyfriend. What else could she expect from such foolishness? What happened to her promise never to repeat this behavior with an unavailable man? Was there something in her psyche that made those men more desirable?

Hours passed as she sat on the couch in a daze. She wanted to cry but the tears never came; only a throbbing lump in her throat persisted. What an idiot she'd been. His *modus operandi* had been revealed to her early on. How could she have missed it? She was a dalliance, a notch on his headboard, just like the rest of the women. She knew women fell in love using their ears; men used their eyes. Wow, he was so good at words.

Along Spain's magnificent highways, she and Miguel had discussed the recklessness – and sheer joy – of their serendipitous affair. What a gift to have found one another as seatmates. But he could have killed her in a far-off hotel room with moonbeams filtering through the window. She could have fled with his possessions or killed him. Their adventure didn't involve morals or poor judgment. Nor was it about *saving one's self for the right partner.* For her, it was the richness of being an older woman making love with a new man. The freedom to seduce Miguel without the promise of tomorrow was an intoxicating risk. But now it was a nightmare, full of shame and disillusionment. It was the classic scenario of how men and women view a casual affair. She's still in the fairy-tale trance; he's checked off another conquest and moved on. With this call, his true self brought her to her knees. Nothing else to do but stand tall, lick her wounds and accept the fact that he did not intend to leave Susan. He'd told Leah that – truthfully. She had to accept it. The first step was to delete his phone number. She'd never contact him again. Next, she had to work on forgetting him. That was the hard part, but she'd do it.

She remembered him talking about the large party he and Susan would host that upcoming weekend. Would he slip and say *we* instead of *I* when he described what he shared with Leah in Spain? How could he make love to Susan and not think about her? Or had she traveled with Miguel in Spain and did someone else live in Virginia?

"I'm known as Mike at home. It's the American nickname for Miguel," he told her on the plane.

"I prefer to call you Miguel. You're not a Mike," Leah

remembered saying.

Writing was her panacea. Her typing fingers often described her own experiences when she invented characters and dialogue. She loved controlling the scenes. But when Miguel left Spain and now, after that dreadful phone call, she needed to control what had happened to her, not to her heroine. Who was Miguel? Who was she with him? How had she been so blindsided? The clues were in his words spoken at the Cuenca café.

This isn't an affair, Leah. This is a love story. You should write about it.

Madrid was unusually rain-soaked during Leah's final week. She stayed home and typed. No canaries chirped anywhere as torrents pounded off the red roof tiles of her once-sunny apartment. As long streaks of rainwater slid down the patio doors to puddle at the thresholds, she was hopelessly lovesick over the brief affair that had vanished – but she kept typing. At night, when the downpours pinged off the metal patio table outside her bedroom window, she envisioned Miguel in bed beside her. She couldn't type then, only hold herself and pretend his arms were around her.

She knew Miguel would never read her beautiful story where she salvaged the best parts and glossed over his ugly words. If nothing else, the exercise was fodder for a future novel, especially the love scenes. Her readers liked them. She kept to her Madrid writing routine except for another dinner with Rocío who seemed eager to know if Miguel had contacted her. She said no. The embarrassment of their last call was too much to reveal just then. Maybe later. Saying he hadn't called reinforced Rocío's low opinion of him.

"Tuck him away. If he reaches out to you, stay away. He's trouble."

Leah was teary-eyed the day she packed for the return flight to New York. The tears rolled down her cheeks in the cab to Barajas Airport. When she clicked shut her seatbelt, the remarkable and unscripted journey she had had with Miguel replayed in her head. Of the three items on her mental agenda when she flew to Spain – reuniting with Javier, changing her approach to men and figuring out how she'd attend Dana's wedding alone – only Javier was done. The other two items seemed to be the mental property of another person. How did they slip away? The *true Leah* would have left Spain renewed and stronger for having worked through her conflicts. The Leah who landed in Spain became the *Id Leah,* a woman fueled by her instinctual impulses, strong enough to satisfy her primitive needs. Her next challenge was to combine the two Leahs in New York and become a fulfilled woman, not the conflicted one buckling in for the return flight.

Javier was definitely yesterday's news she concluded as the plane taxied onto the runway. Her heart closed when she left him in the Salamanca hotel room sitting on the bed in his underwear pleading with her not to leave him. How odd that he still called her cell phone after she left him. She sent his calls to voicemail until he stopped.

As the plane climbed and Spain's coastline vanished under a thick cloud layer, Leah smiled when she thought about the consequences of having shaken hands with her seatmate, the incredible Miguel Santiago. This time when the flight attendant's beverage cart appeared at her row, she refused all drinks. She opened her purse and found the sleeping pill and an eye mask in a zippered pocket, exactly where she'd put them for the trip to Spain. She popped the pill and covered her eyes. The seat beside her was empty. Try as hard as she could to push Miguel's memory to the recesses of her mind, she saw him sitting there. His imagined presence coaxed her right knee to rest against his where it stayed for the long journey across the Atlantic and the return to her New York home.

Leah felt like she received a huge hug from her New York apartment when she turned the key and entered. One large suitcase was left to unpack in the morning. The small computer bag was unzipped and her laptop placed on a desk. Within minutes, the Welcome screen opened. Leah's was addicted to being online. Next, she walked to the entertainment center and turned on the TV. She smiled when she heard English spoken. She poured a glass of Spanish wine, kicked off her shoes holding swollen feet from the long plane ride and plopped her tired body on her semi-circle couch.

An outside terrace stretched along one living room wall and let in a spectacular sunset that wrapped nearby skyscrapers in shades of red, purple and yellow. Other walls held decorative artwork from her travel-writing adventures. The display ranged from carved mahogany Indonesian masks to a goatskin Bodhran Celtic drum. In addition to being beautiful, the art always prompted conversations with her guests. As she admired her two-bedroom apartment decorated in white-to-soft-almond shades, contemporary furniture and towering, leafy-green ferns, Leah succumbed to the comfort of being home.

Her love story with Miguel, written in Spain, remained an unopened Word document.

For about a month, her non-stop New York life consumed

her, but she couldn't shake Miguel's memory. He haunted her, and she hated herself for allowing that. She was weak. She knew he wouldn't call, and he didn't. But why couldn't she lick away his kisses from her lips? Flashbacks of their vivid and erotic lovemaking kept him inside her and ready to climax long after he'd left. She heard his rich baritone voice whispering, *I love you.* Any sane woman would have abandoned those memories from the last shared bed in Spain. Or at least let them evaporate when her suitcases were thrown on the baggage belt for the New York-bound flight.

Because she lived a semi-reclusive life as a writer, Leah forced herself into social activities with men and women that developed into deep and lasting friendships. But she truly enjoyed her women friends. Initially, she planned to keep Miguel a secret, wondering if her friends would find her foolish to have run off with him. They'd wonder if there was a real foundation for a lasting relationship. But what were friends for if not to share experiences?

Leah created fiction and non-fiction travel articles but the Miguel love story came from her heart. The experience of meeting a man on a plane and having it escalate to a hot love affair captivated the imagination of her women friends once she revealed it. Many of the women were close to her age. Some were divorced, while others had never married. Leah rarely socialized with married women. The playing field wasn't level. Slowly, she asked her New York women friends to read the story she'd written about her experience with Miguel in Spain, never expecting their overwhelming and positive feedback. It felt good to release the tale into the larger world.

"Tell me more. How did you reach such a level of sexual freedom with this man? I want what you had with him," her friend Rita said. "I miss romance in my life. You make my heart flutter with this love story."

"I can't explain all of it," Leah said. "We met and the attraction was explosive. I still can't get him out of my mind. He's on my eyelids when I wake up and when I go to sleep."

Rita had lost count of her lovers, finally separating them by decades. But they never stayed around. She wasn't a *femme fatale*, but as she moved into her fifties she wasn't thinking like a virgin either. She talked wistfully about never marrying and now realized she missed an important life event.

"Looks like I forgot to get married and have children. So now I pamper my dog like so many other fifty-something, lonely New York women. You're lucky to have kids, Leah."

As a corporate lawyer, she worked long hours, had plenty of financial assets, enough to care for herself and a man, but he never came along. Unlike Rocío, who was down on men, Rita loved the game.

"That was a ballsy move to run away with a seatmate, Leah. You can teach us all how to go for it. Keep me posted if he calls."

"I don't expect a call, but thanks for reading what I wrote."

Her divorced friend, Vicki, lived in an artist's SoHo loft as a sculptor. Leah adored her mystical qualities. They talked often about the men in their lives. Before Leah's trip to Spain, Vicki advised her to open up her chakras while traveling. "Let in all those physical, mental and emotional interactions," she said.

Google educated Leah about where to find the seven points in her body. They certainly opened when she met Miguel, especially the sacral spot. That corresponded to the sexual and creative center of one's body.

When Vicki read Leah's story, she was creating pink,

ceramic bananas with amorous decals on them, added for a whimsical feminine touch. The fruit forms were to be used for *seductive* healing purposes. The packaging design was still on the drawing board and needed to be sexy.

"Hey, Leah. Would you mind if I used parts of your Segovia love scene with Miguel for the banana-box packaging?" Vicki asked.

"Huh? How do my written words work with bananas?"

"Just say yes. You'll see what I mean. Let me give more exposure to that hot Spanish night the two of you had. Come on, please. You won't be disappointed."

"Okay. Use it. My *love story* with Miguel deserves a boost. Even if it's in a box with a pink ceramic banana," she said and laughed.

When Leah attended Vicki's opening in a lower Manhattan bookstore that also carried erotic art and literature, the Segovia love scene had a new interpretation. Vicki had copied the text onto pink tissue paper and shredded it into long and delicate curly strips. Snippets of Leah's words were still readable. Fluffy bunches of the paper strips were scattered on a tabletop with the $69 pink bananas resting on them. Two college girls, doubling as sales people, had affixed small strips of the shredded paper to their pierced earrings. One dangling curlicue had a description of Leah's erotic remembrance; the other had Miguel's swirling-tongue image.

"So what do you think?" Vicki asked and elbowed Leah. "Great idea. Right?"

"Your talents never cease to amaze me," Leah said with a wide grin.

Vicki took Leah aside as the customers handled the bananas, read the decals, smiled or snickered at the pink creations. Some were purchased.

"Listen to me," Vicki said. "You have to do something big with this Miguel story. It's powerful writing. There's a potent message for women. When I picked up the pink tissue paper from the copy shop, the young girl asked if there were more pages."

"She read them? Isn't that against company policy?"

"Probably, but you wrote some sexy stuff, Leah. It caught her eye. Not only did she read them, she asked for more. How amazing is that? Get the story out there. Like, go for it. A lot of women would appreciate the message."

Following the opening, Vicki invited her list of "Amazing Women" to an intimate dinner at a nearby Mexican restaurant. A lesbian couple arrived late and took their seats at the long table. An overhead spotlight shone directly on them. When Vicki gave the women the banana box, they leaned into one another to open it. The partner with the spiked black hair, black horn-rimmed super-sized eyeglasses and dressed in a black leather jacket with shoulder studs and shiny zippers on many pockets, uncurled one strip of the tissue paper. She softly read Leah's steamy words to her fresh-faced partner with the golden ringlets and tight-fitting floral dress snuggled beside her. They passed the pink ceramic banana between them and smiled.

"Nice stuff you wrote," the woman with the spiked hair said to Leah when Vicki introduced her as the author.

Until then, Leah was simply a friend sipping a frozen margarita and dipping warm tortilla chips into a spicy salsa mix. Three pink bananas in different sizes were stacked in a Bloomingdale's shopping bag at her feet. Vicki had given them to her as a gift for the use of her writing.

"How did you write something like that?" asked the amazed

college student, turned temporary sales person, seated near her. Leah's love-scene curlicues swayed from her earrings. "I love what you wrote. It was, like so real, like I felt I was right there with you and Miguel. But aren't you embarrassed to put your sex life on paper? I couldn't do that. It would show up on my Facebook page. No way would I expose myself like you did. But I admire you for writing it."

Leah was uncomfortable being publicly identified since she'd never written that truthfully about her sex life. But the student was so thirsty for knowledge that Leah straightened up in her chair and gave an older-woman's, sage-like response.

"Oh, it's easy. Forget about Facebook. You young people are too into social networking. Just go home tonight and write the hottest love scene you can remember. Mail it to yourself. The impact will be amazing when you open the letter and read your words. Then share the letter with friends, in person, and get their reactions. Making love is a natural part of life. Romance and lovemaking should be a lifelong enjoyable experience. But be selective; otherwise, men can damage you permanently."

"Thanks for the advice. I'll give it a try tonight but I've never had a boyfriend say things to me that Miguel said to you."

Vicki took Leah aside as she was leaving the restaurant. "Have you sent this story to Miguel?" she asked glaring at Leah.

"No I haven't. But I rework it constantly. Am I trying to keep this affair alive if only on paper? I can't forget him."

"What the hell, Leah. Send it to him. It's beautiful. We all get that you want this over. But rough him up a bit with the truth. He's like a lot of men we've known. No balls. Lots of psycho-babble going on. Broken hearts. Send it to him, please. Let him read what he said. Who knows, maybe this one isn't over yet."

Three empty cabs passed Leah as she stood dazed on the corner of Broadway contemplating Vicki's advice. If she did send Miguel their story, what would it accomplish? A call from him again saying he was so happy to be home with Susan. But it really didn't involve Susan. The Miguel and Leah story was beautiful, sexy, real and his too. He should see it. Her inner voice – or was it her insanity again – hoped it would lure him back to her. If he didn't want her in his life, he'd have to tell her again for it to sink in. She knew at a deep level that he missed her as much as she missed him.

The next day, she retrieved his private phone number from a Post-It she'd stuck on the *Miguel's Abduction* file folder in her desk drawer. That was the story's title.

"Is this the real and sexy Leah Lynch?" he said when she spoke his name.

"It is."

"I'm thrilled you called. How are you? I think of you so often."

"I'm just fine. I think of you, too."

"I have a present for you," he said. "It's a photo album of our trip. I'll send it to you and include several books we discussed during our long drives. Spain would never have been the same without you," he added with a sweet and childlike touch of melancholy in his voice.

"And I have a present for you. Per your suggestion in Cuenca, I wrote our love story. I didn't think I could write so vividly but the words streamed out. There were no notes for reference, only my heart remembering you. Can I send the story to your office?"

"You wrote it? I'm shocked. Of course, send it. I'm honored."

"You still with Susan?" Leah couldn't believe she asked that question.

"Yes. Her best friend from childhood died recently. She really needs my support right now."

"Oh. Sorry to hear that. Our story is in the mail tomorrow. It's called *Miguel's Abduction.*

"Who abducted whom? Is that what it implies?"

"Yes."

Leah read the story multiple times, checking its flow and every comma before she printed Miguel's copy. With each reading, she fell more deeply in love with him – or at least the man he had been in Spain. She didn't know the stateside Mike. But she couldn't acknowledge that in her accompanying note. Instead, she wrote a few perfunctory lines saying she hoped he'd like her efforts. Not trusting the post office, although she did with other manuscripts, Leah went to a FedEx branch and paid extra for a morning delivery.

"I've never received a present like this," Miguel said several days later when he called. "I only skimmed a few pages due to a heavy workload. Your recollection of our exquisite night in Segovia quickly took me back to Spain and being in your arms. I was making love to you in absentia. But I need a quiet office for a full and in-depth read. I'll call you Sunday. I love you, Leah," he said before they hung up.

She forgot to ask what time on Sunday, realizing the omission when she replayed their conversation, ad nauseum, in her lonesome mind as she waited for his private phone number to illuminate her cell phone. That aggravated her since she wasn't accustomed to not having instant contact with him. But it didn't annoy her enough to realize that she'd slipped into second place with Miguel. His Virginia home life came first;

Leah wasn't on his horizon any more, much less in his morning gaze across the pillows. When a sliver of dusk's golden light beamed through her New York apartment window and Miguel hadn't called, she was devastated. By nightfall, she knew his call wouldn't come that day or any other. Miguel had already left her and Spain behind when their love story arrived on his desk in Virginia.

CHAPTER SIX

Two seasons passed with no contact from Miguel and no reaction to *Miguel's Abduction*. Leah had hoped her written words would entice him enough to want to know her more. She wanted a call telling her he still loved her. She wanted him to leave Susan. His snub, his not doing anything, was searing. Eventually, his memory, once such a high, now made her sad as the silence lengthened. But she had to accept the fact that some things in life just didn't tidy up. Somewhere along the line, regaining her sanity, she actually started to admire him for staying away; Susan was obviously still the focus of his love life.

Leah gently asked her girlfriends to stop asking about him. He'd be tucked away in her soul, not to be mentioned on her lips. Simultaneously, she recognized that he'd awakened a deep desire in her to be in love again. Maybe that was his purpose. But how and where would she find that new man? She was growing older. The opportunities to meet someone casually were slipping away along with the ecstasy she'd felt with Miguel. Maybe computer dating was worth a try.

One balmy New York evening, Leah left her girlfriend's apartment in a Midtown hi-rise building headed for a blind date. She was apprehensive. It was her first venture with Match. com. When she reached the lobby and stepped into a pie-wedge section of the revolving door, a deliveryman stepped into another wedge. His strong push put Leah on the sidewalk with a jolt.

She decided to walk the few blocks to the small lounge where she'd meet Gary Collier. New Yorkers were programmed for pavement commutes. Leah liked what the exercise did to firm her thighs. Walking also guaranteed superb spectator time since strange, entertaining people paraded the city's streets. That night, a street person staggered past wearing a heavy coat topped with a makeshift covering of dark-green garbage bags fastened with masking tape. A pungent body odor lingered as he pushed a large, canvas cart filled with cast-off belongings.

A babbling, middle-aged woman approached from another side. Initially, she was presentable, dressed in a powder-blue linen suit. As she hobbled closer on patent-leather spiked heels, Leah noticed her comical face. Layers of dark-brown make-up had been smeared over her sagging skin. Arched eyebrows resembled chocolate-brown boomerangs. The woman's lips were encircled with several shades of lipstick, turning her mouth into a bull's-eye target.

"But, of course, darling, I'd love to have dinner with you," she said as she passed Leah. "Shall we dine at 21 or Four Seasons?"

The walk prepared Leah for the blind date. She visualized Gary driving into Manhattan on the Long Island Expressway. Was he apprehensive, too? They'd met online and agreed to a face-to-face meeting after several weeks of emails. Online dating to find love made her uncomfortable. Was it a new low for her? But the search correlated with everything else she did in her life with her computer: emails, invoices, articles or a novel. Why not find a new man on the Internet? Several days into her search for companionship, she was hooked by the anonymity of surfing for personality choices, all with the click of a mouse.

Gary contacted her first. She liked that he enjoyed dancing. Unbeknownst to him, one of Leah's fantasies took place in a large ballroom where she and her man would twirl, all alone, under colorful frescoes. "Get real," she said when her mind replayed the scene as she walked along Seventh Avenue. He had good phone skills and this was just a first meeting.

Roxie's Lounge in the theater district had double, wooden front doors with gleaming brass plates anchoring the handles. The etched glass inserts depicted caricatures of women from *Chicago*, the Broadway hit. The place took on a warm and cozy glow with its brick walls, long bar and whimsical drawings in mahogany frames. Leah sat at one of the high tables with two stools far enough away from the noisy crowd, perfect for a first meeting.

"I'll be wearing a cap," Gary said when arranging a time. "And I'm about 35 pounds heavier than the online photo. Those pounds just kept packing on before I noticed it. But I've got a great new exercise CD I plan to start using next week."

"Yeah, I know what you mean about pounds. Hope you can lose them, for your sake. It's not healthy at our age." She sensed doom coming.

Overweight was an issue for her. If a man couldn't take care of himself as he aged, she wasn't going to play nursemaid. She was looking for decent looks, good grooming and a terrific personality. The main quality she looked for was courage but why mention that with an initial phone call. Who'd admit to being a wimp? She also needed humor in the equation but that was innate, not learned. Most profiles on the dating sites listed "a sense of humor" as important, which she found silly. Who'd want a grump? She'd know early on if Gary could tell a funny story or simply react to one. And he'd have to be a great lover. Character, honesty and valor were important, too. Her friends had those attributes but she didn't sleep with them.

"Maybe we can dine at the restaurant if the night works out," Gary mentioned.

Leah took that remark as secret-code talk. If there were chemistry, they'd continue in the dining room. *Cheap bastard. Why not have dinner anyway?*

"A glass of Merlot," she said to the waitress as the front door opened and a man wearing a cap walked in. A friend told her never to give a truthful description of herself when meeting a blind date at a bar. She should check him out first. Test her intuition. If she didn't like him, she could leave undetected. Not a bad idea Leah thought, as the man in the checkered cap smiled and walked toward her.

"Leah? Leah Lynch?" he asked nervously.

"You must be Gary," she said faking a warm smile and extending her hand.

Instantly, she felt uneasy as he swiped his hat off and stuffed it in his back pocket. She avoided a long first glance because she didn't want her disappointment to show. *Not a good vibe here.* Maybe by evening's end that would change. After settling in his chair, Leah noticed large rolls of fat under and above his belt. He reminded her of Tweedle Dum, or was it Tweedle Dee? She tried to overlook his size since, in time, most people had something that sagged or protruded. But why put *slender* on his profile?

A hush fell over Leah and Gary, the ever-awkward beginning

of new conversations. When words finally came, they started slowly.

"How was your ride into the city?"

"Not bad but I prefer living on Long Island. Never warmed up to Manhattan. I'll have a Bud," he said when the waitress approached.

The small table candle flickered its image in Gary's old-fashioned eyeglasses. When Leah ran her manicured finger over the candleholder's rim, his eyes followed. His tongue traveled the curve of his upper lip. She withdrew her hand. He was in his late fifties, divorced and had a grown son.

"I guess you could say I neglected him as a kid. Just too much for me to handle. He's grown now. I kind of like him again."

"Sounds like a callous parenting job to me," Leah said, surprised at her straightforward response. Since she didn't want to reveal much of her past, she groped for subjects to share with him. Not everyone knew her as a stay-at-home housewife who car-pooled with the other mothers, baked for cake sales, went house-to-house collecting for charities and led a bland existence until she left it behind one day. And not all men liked independent women.

"You come and go too much," one man said on a date. "Most men would be afraid to start a long-standing relationship. There's nothing permanent about you."

As Gary and Leah's conversation dragged on, he boasted about past girlfriends loving the beef stroganoff he cooked for them. He hinted its success usually led to their staying the night.

Out! Out! Out was all Leah wanted from the dreadful computer date. *Maybe I should get right off this stool and bolt out the door?*

"It's a long day tomorrow," she said gulping down the last of her wine. "I'm calling it a night. You can stay and finish your beer if you like. I'll walk myself home."

"I'll walk you home. You're really nice," he said and signaled for the check, looking at her handbag, which implied he thought she'd share the cost. She didn't.

As they walked along Seventh Avenue, he listed his dance-floor skills and hinted at his prowess in bed. When they reached her apartment building, Leah rummaged for her keys and put the large one in the upper lock. Gary put his hand on the door as if to walk in with her.

"Ah, good night, Gary," she said and stopped abruptly. "It was a pleasure to meet you. I wish you well with computer dating, but we're not for one another."

"What do you mean? We're getting along just fine."

"Maybe for you, but not for me. And you lied on Match. You look much older than your photos. You're heavier than slender. We have nothing in common. But thanks for the wine."

"Hey, look. We all lie on Match. One woman showed up and I didn't recognize her at all. She used her daughter's photo in her bio."

When she extended her hand, he was taken aback but returned the gesture. She hoped her cool good-bye signaled a lack of further interest.

"Good night, Leah," he said squeezing her hand while cupping it with his other hand. "I hope to see you again. I'll call."

She smiled and withdrew her hand, waiting for him to leave before she opened the front door. *All he wants is sex*, Leah thought, as she waited for the elevator. She felt alone, dejected and lost in the dating game. It never did please her. What a disappointing evening. At least she knew what she didn't want in a man. Her intuition had held up. Leah turned both locks in her apartment door, glad to be home alone. She avoided turning on the lights. She courted darkness that evening. The telephone blinked several messages that she ignored.

In the moonlit darkness, she unbuttoned her blouse, unhooked her bra, unzipped her skirt and slithered out of the clothes, letting them pile on the floor. She reached into a bureau drawer, pulled out black cotton leggings and yanked a long-sleeved shirt over her head; her uniform for relaxing at home.

"What a creep. Jerk. He wants a fast lay," she mumbled as she walked over to stretch out on the couch and stare into the New York sky. Thousands of window lights in hundreds of apartments met her gaze. The stillness around her was wonderful as she inhaled and exhaled solitude. Closing her eyes that had begun to tear, she bolted upright when the intercom rang.

"Don't tell me he's back," she said walking slowly to the intercom. When it buzzed again, she hesitated. Answer it or not? She picked up the handset.

"Who is it?"

"Hi Mom. I left several messages. Can I come up?"

"Of course you can. My door is always open for my beautiful daughter."

"Mom, how come your clothes are on the floor? That's not like you," Dana said when she went into the bedroom to put her coat on Leah's bed. She then joined her mother on the couch.

"Awful blind date, honey. I came home feeling sorry for myself. I didn't notice I dropped my clothes. Let's not discuss me. How are the wedding plans going?"

"Mostly good but I need your help Mom."

"Okay, let's make our To Do List. It's so exciting to see you becoming a bride."

For the next two hours, she and her daughter planned the day, the menu and surveyed the ever-growing guest list. So many people knew Leah as Mrs. McCord. She didn't want to see them again, but she couldn't tell her daughter the emotion was growing as the wedding neared.

"Are you attending the wedding with anyone, Mom?"

"No. Just me that day. I wish I had someone special, but I don't."

"Do you want Steve and me to find someone for you? He knows plenty of single men at the hospital who can accompany you. It can be hush-hush and just between the three of us. Interested?"

"No, I'm fine, honey. I'm attending alone. How about a cup of tea?" she asked abruptly to distract from the uncomfortable subject.

"Sure if you're having one."

Leah excused herself from the couch and went into the kitchen. She didn't want Dana to see her tears welling up. Was she a failure in her daughter's eyes because she didn't have a man in her life? What would those old street friends say about her attending alone?

A recent conversation with Melanie, a long-standing Rhode Island friend, came to mind as Leah prepared tea and cookies. Dana was texting while she waited on the couch for her mother.

"Hey, Leah. What's up here?" Melanie asked when they discussed the wedding. "How come no steady boyfriend or another husband?"

"Not yet. I'm a collector of affections until he comes along," Leah said, masking her truth of the last few years that she really did want a man in her life.

"That's a good one. 'A collector of affections.' You must have a big stash by now. Are you bringing one of those collectibles to the wedding?"

"You'll see," Leah said, knowing she had no one to invite. She particularly dreaded the first dance. Maybe she'd hire a date from an escort agency, requesting someone younger. He'd be dashing and capable of making the other women envious. "He's my latest," she'd tell everyone with a wink. "Nothing like a drop-dead-gorgeous younger lover until the right man comes along," she'd add. Maybe she'd pay him more to be extra attentive. Money was no longer an issue for her. She had the nerve to hire a date but that was so unlike her. She was a woman renown for handling touchy situations with bravery and honesty. Showing up with a fake beau at her daughter's wedding was a desperate act. But that conversation took place before Leah went to Spain and met Miguel. Amazing how a chance meeting can change one's world. Now she only wanted him beside her and forever.

"Dana, how do you take your tea?" Leah yelled into the living room. "Sugar, or are you sweet enough?"

"No sugar, Mom. Just lemon and what does that tell you about me?"

Leah returned to the couch carrying a bone-china serving tray decorated with pink, lavender and blue hydrangeas. The fancy souvenir originated from Stoke-on-Trent where Leah had researched and written a travel article about English china and pottery. Two dainty matching cups held steaming Earl Grey tea.

"You're such a special and beautiful lady, Mom. How come you never married again?" Dana asked and startled Leah with her abrupt question.

"I never wanted another marriage, honey. Also, raising two children from a distance took away any serious search. All the travel I did, all the solitude needed for writing novels and, yes, all the affairs didn't exactly work well with marriage or help me find anyone who stayed that long. We both remember the brief engagement with Sal but let's forget it, too. No regrets, sweetie. I'm a happy woman today, but it's harder as we age to find the right man. Dates simply don't come around that fast. Does it bother you that I don't have someone to invite to your wedding? Tell me the truth, Dana."

"It doesn't bother me if it doesn't bother you, Mom. Now that I'm about to be a wife, I can only imagine the pain you suffered when your marriage didn't work. I'd be devastated to think I couldn't live out my life with Steve. When I was younger, I was your daughter. Sitting beside you now, I'm your friend, too. I've told you before how much I love and respect you. I'm saying it again. Few women could have accomplished what you did. You taught me how to be an empowered woman. "Thank you," Dana said with misted eyes.

"Leaving our home was the hardest decision I've ever made. But I had your father's blessing. It was difficult, for sure, but it was best for everyone. Working through the divorce was a long process. Dad and I are better parents. But no more talk about the past. Let's plan this glorious wedding of yours."

"To the big day," Leah said and raised her teacup to gently touch her daughter's.

Leah couldn't tell her daughter she didn't want to attend the wedding alone. How ridiculous, shallow and self-centered she'd sound. She shouldn't be dragged into her mother's obsession about returning to their home state without a man. Instead, Leah kept their conversation upbeat and full of laughter. She grilled Dana about every minute wedding detail. When they came to the issue of money, Leah said not to worry. "It's under control. All you have to think about is looking beautiful and spending the rest of your life with your husband."

"You're an incredible mother," Dana whispered into Leah's ear when they hugged longer than usual as she prepared to leave.

"I am who I am because you loved and understood me long before I understood myself," Leah said and held in a sob.

When Dana left, Leah dialed her ex-husband's telephone number. She knew it from memory.

"Jim," she said without much expression in her voice when he answered. "Dana stopped by my apartment tonight. We discussed her wedding."

"She's pretty excited, isn't she?"

"You and I were, too, about our wedding. But that was eons ago. How's your wife Sun-Hee and your little boy?"

"We're all fine. Max is a holy terror. Never stops."

"Good. I'm glad everything's working out. I know we agree the divorce brought unnecessary pain to our children," Leah said, jumping to the call's purpose. "But they still turned into fine adults. Dana's wedding day should be everything she wants it to be."

"Yes, we did hurt them so let's try to work out this wedding as best as possible. And I want to thank you for divorcing me," he added. "These past few years have been the best of my life."

"My pleasure. Not being Mrs. McCord has been wonderful for me, too. I'm going to make the financial planning easy for us," Leah said with a commanding voice. "How about you pay for Dana's dress and I'll pick up the rest of the expenses including an open bar." Her life after their divorce and leaving Rhode Island had been successful. Her novels were bestsellers and money stopped being an issue. Dana shouldn't pay for anything.

"That's very generous, Leah. Are you sure?"

"I'm positive. We don't need a meeting or any more calls. See you at Dana's wedding. It will be a fine day."

When they hung up, Leah felt a trance overcome her. Her hometown street and her early-married days unfolded as she stared into space. The McCord's first purchase was a home on Williston Avenue in an idyllic middle-class New England neighborhood. The neighbors waved as they passed, shoveled their sidewalks, trimmed summer lawns and raked leaves into large trash bags. At Christmastime, their evergreen and azalea bushes glowed with lights. The McCords fit right in.

She remembered how hard she fell for Jim from the minute they met in their high school cafeteria. After three years of lustful dating, she bequeathed her virginity to him. A year later, they married and naively planned their Rhode Island lives. While others viewed their marriage as idyllic, it was too painful for Leah to endure. When she called it quits, her harsh and quick decision to leave Rhode Island surprised everyone. Even her best friend, Melanie, didn't know about Leah's plan to move to New York when she pulled into the McCord driveway. She thought they were going to the mall.

"What's up here?" Melanie asked as Leah threw two suitcases in the back seat.

"I'll tell you later. Come on, let's go," she muttered and slammed the car door shut.

"What's the hurry, Leah?"

"I'll tell you later. Let's go."

Their neighbor, Miss Northup, dragged a rusty metal rake across her dying lawn as they drove past. The rhythmic strokes sent leaves through the bow of her legs. Aged and bundled in the black coat she wore to her friends' funerals, she glanced up from her leaves and stopped to rest wrinkled fingers on her rake. She waved as they passed. Leah returned the gesture knowing she'd no longer be a decaying soul on that street.

"Why are you crying like this?"

"We're not going to the mall. My marriage is over. I'm leaving the house and moving to New York to become a writer. I'm scared, Melanie."

"What? You're what?"

"I can't continue lying to myself. I have to make this move."

"I don't know how you can do this," Melanie said, aghast at her friend's unforeseen departure. She always supported Leah but this wrenching decision baffled her. "You'll be sorry. Mothers don't desert their children and run off trying to create a career," she said. "Please rethink this. Let's go to lunch. We'll talk," Melanie pleaded.

"Take me to the airport. Be the friend I need and not a therapist."

Leah then reminded her about the conversation Melanie overheard between her mother-in-law and her sister. The two frail elderly women rocked on Melanie's front porch one summer day, their feet barely touching the wooden boards.

"Do you remember when I worked as an extra on the *Gone with the Wind* set?" one sister asked the other.

She did.

"And do you remember when Clarke Gable asked me to

lunch?"

The sister remembered.

"Well," she said sadly, "I should have gone."

Melanie's simple story about her relatives made Leah vow she'd never rock her life away and say, *"I should have gone."*

"What a life it turned out to be," Leah said aloud sitting alone in her New York apartment. She had it all now: successful career; loving and educated children; ex-husband was happily remarried with a new life; world travel; wonderful friends; she had, she had, she had. What Leah suspected she didn't have was the courage needed to confidently return to her past and attend Dana's wedding, especially without a committed man standing by her side.

CHAPTER SEVEN

ONE OF LEAH'S FAVORITE New York City pastimes was brunch with friends. It was a balmy Sunday in May, and she was in a great mood when she prepared for the monthly occasion. Just before leaving her apartment, she closed the terrace doors as a delightful breeze filtered through the sheer, full-length window panels that billowed into space.

Despite being late, but out of habit, she stopped at her mailbox in the building's vestibule. Normally, she'd shuffle through the contents and return them for a later retrieval. That day, bank statements and junk mail stood upright alongside an oversized postcard. It was rare to receive personal mail since emails had replaced handwritten messages that conveyed the thought and protected the sender. The card's colorful front showed a busy medieval main square with a battle scene. Equestrians sat upright on reared stallions with flared nostrils. In the distance, lush pastures surrounded a stone church with a bell tower. Leah's heart began to beat rapidly. She knew the sender.

Hola Leah,

I'm in Italy. You came along since I can't forget you. What happened to us was true and ours forever. I'm adverse to duplicity and dare to bare my feelings because I'm once more in the Promised Land. I hope you are well and prospering. I am sure you are.

Love, Miguel

Leah froze in place with the postcard in her hand. She reread his message several times, enough to memorize every word. She turned the card from front to back. She ran her fingers over the airmail stamp. She tried to decipher the postmark's time and date. *I know he loves me. I know he can't stay away. I love him, too. Why can't we be grownups? Why a silly postcard with a deeply personal message? Why didn't he call me? Why didn't he invite me to travel with him?*

Seven months had slipped by without any acknowledgement of the story she wrote for them. Seven months of an undeserved and nasty snub. Now Miguel was in her hands via a simple postcard. A confusing hot flash of emotion rushed through her. She had rationalized his silence to mean he wanted his mundane routine in Virginia. He rejected her.

When her heart finally accepted the rejection, she tucked him away in a Miguel Memory Box brimming with Spain flashbacks and his private telephone number attached to certain days and times to call. She also had his home address, which she had copied from his luggage tag. When she returned to New York, she downloaded Google Earth and zeroed in on his home. An in-ground swimming pool was off a back deck and surrounded by acres of woodland. A Mercedes was in the driveway. She envisioned Miguel going from room to room. Susan was never in those scenes nor did Leah picture them in bed. Taking the hunt for his address that far made her feel sleazy, but she forgave herself by saying that she was simply curious. Most writers are.

Eventually, Leah accepted the passage of time without Miguel. It was a daily mental erosion until his physical image faded from her mind. Meeting him on a plane was an exquisite adventure but to continue the after-Spain bliss was madness. So she dropped the daydreams and continued with her all-consuming New York life that included finishing her latest romance novel. The hectic pace meant endless meetings with her editor and long quiet nights revising her manuscript. She also made frequent trips to Rhode Island as she and Dana visited venues for the upcoming wedding.

Receiving Miguel's postcard confirmed what her heart knew all along. He missed her. He loved her. He had to stay in touch. What would or should she do? Confused by the moment, Leah couldn't cram his postcard back into the mailbox between the junk mail and bills. Instead, she slipped the card into her purse, slung it over her shoulder and clutched his words to her heart. Miguel would accompany her, in absentia, for the day.

She didn't reveal Miguel's postcard to her brunch friends. When she returned home, she left it in her purse, occasionally sneaking a peek at his loving words. How to stay occupied and not think about him consumed the rest of her day. Although a housekeeper had cleaned her apartment thoroughly, Leah vacuumed all the rugs and even the baseboards. At dusk, she walked to Central Park, finding her favorite spot above the Pond. The Ramble consisted of thirty-six secluded acres, intersecting footpaths, a tiny stream and dense foliage. About two hundred species of birds inhabited the park with many perched on nearby branches. Amidst their chirps, Leah sat on a bench and watched boaters dip their oars in the Pond creating mesmerizing ripples. The bewildering question of how to handle Miguel stayed with her. By bedtime, an answer wasn't coming so she slipped his card under her pillow.

By morning, the longing to see him again overpowered her sensibility to ignore the card. She lay in bed dwelling on his cheap trick to express his desire for her. A rush of anger and hurt surfaced where it hadn't the day before. She wanted a do-or-die moment with him, akin to a face-off. Was he that naïve to think a miss-you-and-still-love-you postcard from Italy erased his cruel rejection of their love story? A story he had suggested and asked to read? Months had passed without even a call.

His message implied he still lived with Susan. Based on that assumption, Leah wanted him out of her life. The more she dwelled on the petty way he had reached out to her, the more she knew it'd be child's play to call him in his office with a flip message to get lost. She'd elevate the confrontation. Why not meet him at a New York airport when he returned from Italy? Miguel needed to connect from his international flight to a national one to fly to Virginia. But which airport – three served the city. What flight? What day? It could be impossible to single him out in a huge airport. What if he hadn't traveled alone and Susan was with him?

"Am I crazy? Am I a stalker?" she'd asked herself. "Hell no. I'm pissed at him, and big time," she'd answer.

Following her imaginary dots and the postcard's date of mailing, she assumed he probably sent it the day he arrived in Italy. He'd be in his European mindset and thought about Leah on the plane. How could he forget? His normal vacation time was two weeks. She guessed he'd fly back from Rome, the origin of the postcard. Leah dialed his office with that revelation.

"Good morning," she said in her best professional voice. "May I speak to Miguel Santiago?"

"Who's calling please?"

"Maryanne Flanders. He asked me to make an appointment."

"Sorry but he's out of the office until a week from Monday. Can I take a message?"

"No thank you. I'll call later."

Bingo. Leah calculated he'd return to Virginia on a Saturday and rest up Sunday. He'd fly the same airline carrier they'd flown to Spain. His international flight would arrive at Newark Airport where he'd transfer to a domestic one. Slowly and with ten days to construct a plan, she became convinced she'd find him. She was positive he had traveled to Italy alone. Susan never went to the Promised Land with him.

"I'm very disappointed in you. Why this approach? Are you desperate for a man?" Rocío scolded. Leah knew she'd have a strong opinion when she called her for advice. "What you propose is insane. How can you find this Miguel, who is now your fantasy lover, at Newark Airport with thousands of people around? It's difficult enough to find someone who's expecting to be found. Don't do it. Please. You'll make a fool of yourself if you do find him," Rocío continued. "Exactly what is your purpose here?"

"My purpose? We love one another and should be together. He doesn't know what to do with that love except send me a postcard. Aging men become unsure of what to do with new women. They lose their bravado, their strength and sometimes their libido. What's left is their tenderness. If I find him, I'll help him reach out to me differently."

"Sentimental and foolish talk, Leah. Don't you see he only loves the chase? He chooses his prey carefully – middle-aged women, divorced, financially secure, with children and craving tenderness – and then he devours them. He infiltrates fragile minds and vulnerable hearts with his deception. You're too smart for this game. Be very careful with this man."

"Do you have to be so blunt?" Leah said.

"He's a lover only, whether past or present. He's not serious about you. He's serious about the affair. Supposedly, you don't want those any more. Why hasn't he left his girlfriend? Think about that fact when you organize your crazy thoughts. And think about something else. Are you serious about him or are you creating material for a new novel?"

"I can't answer your astute questions. The novel part crossed my mind, too. But I do love him. I can't stop thinking about him. He's in my heart. He makes me hot even in my dreams. We're destined to meet at the airport."

"Incredible thinking on your part, Leah. Well, you'll do exactly what you want to do. I'm sure of that. Prepare yourself for a disastrous heartbreak with this man. If he's the one, I tip my hat for your courageous and unending approach. Maybe he does love you, after all. You, the flight to Spain, Segovia and everything else you two did should be long gone from his memory by now," Rocío said with a hint of sweetness in her voice. "Now on to more realistic topics. Tell me about the wedding. I plan to attend. I've never been to New England and look forward to seeing the smallest state."

"Plans are full speed ahead. Dana invited me to choose

her wedding dress with her. What a magical day we had, pure mother and daughter togetherness. As soon as she put it on, we knew it was the one. I cried myself to sleep. But you're making me sentimental right now. Time to go. We'll talk again, and soon. I'm sure you'll want to know if I found Miguel at the airport or chickened out and stayed home. *Hasta luego.*"

A Newark Airport security guard directed a noticeably nervous Leah to the area outside the door for Terminal B's Arrivals. It was mayhem as hundreds of passengers from other international flights streamed out of the doorway. The scene resembled a stampede. Passengers going to New York City and beyond went to her left. Connecting passengers entered a narrow, glass-enclosed corridor leading to other terminals. Miguel would be among them since his flight to Virginia departed from Terminal C.

Leah paced in front of the glass. It was an almost-impossible winnowing down since her subjects moved quickly. She looked for men who matched Miguel's stature. When her eyes blurred, she scanned those with a similar gait. *Oh my god, what will I do if he sees me first? He'll think I'm a crazed woman. What am I doing at Newark Airport scoping out a lover? Turn around and go home, you idiot. Stop this asinine behavior before it's too late.*

When a priest appeared, followed by two nuns and a lanky teenager wearing an *Italia* T-shirt, she knew his flight from Rome had arrived. Intense apprehension overcame her; her hands were clammy and ice cold. Suppose her ridiculous plot worked? What would he think? Never mind his opinion. She was worth the embarrassment of a confrontation. No more rejection-prone men calling her months later or sending postcards.

Her tired feet swelled in her shoes after a two-hour wait. No Miguel. Hoards of new passengers streamed through Customs' doors and convinced her that she'd probably missed him. Disheartened, feeling like a jerk, barely able to accept her failure and with zero options left, she decided to go home.

Few people remained in the long terminal when she retraced her steps to the outside platform where she'd take the bus back to Manhattan. She felt very alone. With her head pounding and dragging broken dreams behind her, she noticed an airline employee open an office door several feet in front of her and walk into the terminal. She waited for him to approach, internally propelled to give the Miguel quest one last try.

"Excuse me," she said and surprised the man, oblivious to a woman in despair. "Can you find out if my friend landed from Rome? I waited for hours in Terminal B for him to transfer to his flight to Virginia, but I must have missed him."

"Is he a special friend?" he asked, which she thought was a strange response. The employee was middle-aged with curly gray hair and his reading glasses rested at the tip of his nose. He had a kind and sympathetic look.

"Very, very special," she replied with the emphasis on *special.* "This day was supposed to be a wonderful surprise for him."

"Follow me," he said as he walked over to a nearby ticket counter.

Leah practically yelped with joy right in the middle of the terminal when he typed in Miguel's name. *Isn't this against the rules?*

"He arrives tomorrow. Not today," the man said matter-of-factly as he ran his finger across the computer screen and looked at her.

"Tomorrow? But I thought it was today."

"Come back then. Request a guest gate pass at this counter. The airline rep might give you one so you can get to his domestic gate," the man continued. When she didn't answer, he shut off the computer and walked away.

During the bus ride home, Leah was stunned to realize she had almost succeeded in her scheme. But should she return the next day? This was all so silly. Was she turning into a *Fatal Attraction* woman? Not really. She only wanted to see Miguel again. She knew the airport layout; the Arrivals' gate procedures; where to stand; how to go from Terminal B to Terminal C for his Virginia flight and how to get a guest gate pass. What began as a simple postcard from Italy had grown into an elaborate plan to confront him at Newark Airport. She was on a pre-destined path. But could she do the airport vigil again, now that she knew she'd actually find him?

Leah boarded the Newark Airport bus the next morning with trepidation, a sign that she was having cold feet. However, an internal drive to find Miguel trumped her fear. She couldn't stay home knowing he'd fly overhead, land a few miles away and be gone. Her scheme to find him was doable. She needed a quick eye, tenacity and courage, lots of it. If he could enter her life unexpectedly again with a postcard from Italy, she'd rock his world with a surprise visit at the airport.

A multi-car accident along the highway squeezed several lanes into one. The air conditioning on the bus wasn't working. Beads of perspiration dripped between Leah's breasts. She wanted to go home. As the bus inched along, her eyes darted between the snarled traffic and her watch. She called the airline and his flight had landed. *Oh my God, all this planning and I'm stuck in traffic.* Deep breaths calmed her, as she remembered it took about an hour to pass through Customs.

Finally, the haggard busload of passengers disembarked and entered Terminal B. Hundreds of people milled about. Hired drivers with passengers' names printed in large letters on hand-held signs awaited their riders. Where to stand, this time unnoticed, as Miguel would pass through the long glass corridor. Close to its exit point, she noticed a wide pole with concave sides. She pressed her body against one curve and wished she'd worn sunglasses and a wide, floppy hat as a partial disguise. It was the perfect spot to see the passengers' backs en route to the escalator. *I'm going to pass out. Dear God, help me through this. Am I crazy? No. I'm just a lovesick middle-aged woman with grown children and I'm hopelessly in love with this man.*

The nearby wall clock ticked away an hour. No Miguel in sight. Her heart grew weary, yet again. Hundreds of passengers passed on their way to the escalator but Miguel wasn't among them. How would she approach him? Her surprise was gigantic, too personal to share with strangers. During the second hour of her vigil, the connecting number of passengers dwindled, as did her hope.

Then, in a flash, out of the corner of her eye, the moving shadow of a solitary man passed within several feet of where she stood. She turned slightly to look at him as he headed toward the empty escalator, rolling one suitcase and hoisting a small carry-on over his shoulder. His gait, similar to a steady glide, was familiar. Her eyes recognized his back; her hand had followed its curve while Spanish moonbeams bounced off his soft skin. She knew his body as the naked one she adored lying beside her. His leather jacket was the one he wore on chilly Spanish nights as they strolled along cobblestone streets and she slipped her arm into his. She knew this man. He was Miguel Santiago, the love of her life.

She expected her heart to pound when she saw him. It didn't. She had envisioned paralysis overtaking her. That didn't happen either. Instead, her steady eyes followed him as he approached the escalator. It was her last chance to run away, forsaking her truth for a coward's safety net. The word *stalker* again crossed her mind.

Instead of slipping out the terminal door and going home, she watched as Miguel stepped onto the escalator, grabbed the handrail and rode in solitude. When he neared the top, she put her foot on the escalator's first step. Pounding heartbeats drowned out all terminal sounds around her. Deep breaths heaved in her chest and kept her focused. Exhales whispered *I love you* between her parted lips. She could have called out his name but chose not to break the numbing spell. About five seconds passed as she rode behind him, enough time for their entire history to become flashcard images in her erotic mind.

Throughout the execution of her airport plan, Leah had had many imaginary conversations with him. Not one came to mind as he stepped off the escalator and looked upward for the Monorail sign to Terminal C. Seconds later, she stood beside him, placed her hand on his arm and gave it a tug.

"It's this way to Terminal C, Miguel. Follow me," she said sweetly.

He lowered his eyes from the sign and pulled his arm away, annoyed at the distraction of being touched. That is, until he recognized the woman beside him.

"Leah. Leah. Leah," he gasped as he backed up in bewilderment. "Oh my God. Is it really you?"

"Yes, it's really me," she said and stood stoically, courageously and dry-eyed. Sheer joy washed over her face. She was a Vermeer painting, reflecting the glow of light Miguel created in her soul.

"How did you do this?" he said when he opened his arms, stepped forward and hugged her harder than she imagined he would. "I still love you, Leah," he whispered. She trembled when he buried his head in her neck. She sought refuge in his arms. Three seasons had passed since they'd seen one another. His eyes told her nothing had changed.

"Well," he said sounding businesslike, baffled at what to do next. "Shall we get a coffee over there?"

"No, of course not. Let's go to your other terminal and be together before you continue on to Virginia," she said and pointed to the Monorail. She really wanted to point him in the direction of New York. Once inside the train's small compartment, she could feel his breath on her face.

"I sent you a postcard from Italy. Did you receive it?"

"That's why I'm here. Don't you understand? Your postcard is why I'm here, Miguel."

Leah confessed to calling his office, connecting the clues, taking a risk to find him and to being at the airport the day before. Large *cojones* helped, too. "Change your flight to a later one so we can visit for a while. We need to talk," she suggested as they traveled down an escalator.

"I can't. I missed my flight yesterday. Susan will meet me. Any more changes will raise suspicion."

Those death-knell and piercing words were not what Leah wanted. She almost gagged with the intensity of her internal pain. Instead, she feigned agreement. *Dear God, rescue me. I'm such a fool to have done this. He's really committed to Susan. How do I get out of this, now that the surprise is over? Did he miss his plane because he met a woman in Italy and didn't want to leave her? He's capable of that.*

When they reached Terminal C's main floor, Miguel led her outside where they formed a cocoon of intimacy beside the revolving doors. The afternoon air was muggy. Leah began to sweat. Nearby, taxi doors thumped shut, passengers rolled their suitcases and families held children in tow as they entered the terminal.

"Why did you ignore me after I wrote our story and sent it to you? I waited for your call," Leah said blurting out her hurt.

"I didn't know what to say. We can't be just friends. What happened to us was a love story, not an affair." He couldn't call her to discuss books, movies or to carry on trivial conversations. He couldn't be duplicitous with a girlfriend at home.

"You hurt me deeply. You were cruel."

Miguel winced.

"And you're still with Susan? Why?"

"I'm afraid to leave. I'm too old for this game. I've left so many women. I start loving them but then something changes. The next one doesn't work out either. If I leave Susan, I'm doomed to failure. I'm positive of that. She's a sweet woman. I guess it's not that bad. She expects me to marry her next year." He avoided Leah's eyes.

On one of the escalators they took that day, Miguel kissed Leah's lips with a childlike peck. Outside the terminal and after he confessed his fears, he wrapped his arms around her and embraced her repeatedly. If they were teenage lovers with backpacks at their feet, his public and powerful embraces might have appeared normal. But theirs wasn't a typical airport kiss; they were middle-aged adults with a few wrinkles to prove it.

"I'm here today to face you with my truth. You have to live alone if you want me in your life. I love you, Miguel," Leah said, surprised at her clarity. "I can easily transport my career to Virginia with a flash drive and a computer. I'll stay with you for a week at a time. You can visit New York. It's all doable. We won't be a *couple.* We'll find another word."

"I'm not engaged," he said, thinking aloud. "I'm not married either nor do I have children to educate. But I do have family commitments and a business to run. You're beautiful and I love you, but I'm in so deep in Virginia? How can I get out?" he asked as his shoulders slumped.

Leah saw a slight tearing in his eyes. Baby tears, not yet grown up. She was emotionally incapable of deciphering his truths from lies; duplicity from decisive action or adulthood from boyish behavior. She knew he was a decent, warm and caring man, not a skirt chaser, just a flawed human being who couldn't embrace all truths. Standing before him saying what she needed was new for her. Her heartfelt words had the potential to destroy the ultimate free-spirited lover she'd been for years. Was she looking for a commitment from Miguel? Yes.

They decided to forego her guest gate pass since his flight would depart in thirty minutes. Instead, they said a quick good-bye when Leah walked him to the security checkpoint, both too much in shock to say what they'd do next. A higher level of self-esteem buoyed her as she walked away. Her mission was complete. She congratulated herself on having the courage to face him. Plus, to single him out at the crowded airport was paramount to a lover's miracle.

Dark, rain-soaked clouds swirled overhead as the New York-bound bus pulled away from the curb to take Leah home. Large raindrops bounced off its roof, like the taps on a drum, reminding her of the torrents in Spain when she and Miguel parted. She surmised he wouldn't fly because of the storm.

Back in her apartment, she checked his flight on her computer. It was rescheduled for an 11:00 p.m. departure, hours away. She didn't know his cell phone number; she accepted his inevitable departure. But there was now an ultimatum on the table, sort of.

"What do you want to do, Miguel?" Leah asked with his surprise call.

"I want to see you. The next flight leaves in several hours. There's enough time to take a cab into the city."

"Come to my apartment. We shouldn't be crammed in with New Yorkers and tourists in a public place," Leah gushed. "But don't take a cab. Too much rain. Take the AirTrain. It stops at Penn Station. I'll meet you under the large Departures' board. We'll take the subway to my place, have a bite to eat and make love for dessert. Like that plan?"

"Oh my God, Leah. I can't wait."

When she arrived at the train station, hundreds of stranded passengers stared at the overhead Departures' board. Miguel wasn't in the crowd. An announcement bellowed through the large hall that all trains between Newark Airport and New York were delayed due to an electrical problem. *No. No. It can't be. We're destined to be together tonight. Please, no.*

"I had to get off the stalled train and return to the airport," his message said on her cell phone. "I couldn't miss the last plane to Virginia. I'm so sorry, Leah. I tried."

"You're a joy to be with," he said still reeling from her surprise visit when she answered his call from the airport.

"Why did you miss your flight the day before? Who's the *chica* you met in Italy that delayed your trip home?" she asked him. "Just call me a good witch. I imagine you not spending your last night alone. I know your game plan."

"*Chica?* Come on now. There wasn't anyone in my bed that last night except me. I missed my flight because I didn't judge the traffic properly in Rome. I should have. Maybe it was a subliminal message. I didn't want to go home. There's nothing to return to in Virginia," he said with resignation. "Seeing you for just one night isn't enough. I want seven nights with you in New York. I want us to travel together." His list of what he wanted them to do trailed off into a clandestine world she didn't want with him nor understand.

"Until next time," he said in Spanish as his flight was called.

"I love you, Miguel. Make the next time soon."

Over the next few months, they talked regularly. He told Leah he was in his office and alone with his feet up on the desk and pressing the phone to his ear to hear her voice as closely as possible.

"Don't live with anyone, Leah," he said one day.

She had no intention to do that.

"I don't want to be domesticated," he said with another call. It was happening.

"I'm living way over my salary," he admitted with another.

"We're going out with the same friends once a month," he lamented, adding that he drank and ate too much to compensate for the boredom.

"Oh, the tyranny of monogamy," he sighed one day. "How can I be true to myself and still respect the woman I live with?"

"Start with honesty."

"We laugh a lot don't we," he said. "You understand me."

She did. But he was in Virginia saying those words, and she wasn't.

CHAPTER EIGHT

IT WAS ONE HOUR BEFORE MIDNIGHT. Leah was sitting in Madrid's Chamartin Train Station waiting to board the *Lusitania*. She'd sleep on the overnight train and arrive in Lisbon, Portugal, the following morning. The rapid clicks on the Departures' board moved the train closer to an assigned track but not fast enough for her. She was exceptionally anxious to board. Rather than sit out the wait, she walked the length of the huge station. Although not thirsty, she dropped a euro into a vending machine, heard the water bottle clunk into the dispensing area and put it into her purse. The buttery scent of croissants drew her to a bakery where she slid another euro across the counter to purchase one with a shimmering glaze. She tucked that purchase into an outside pocket on her suitcase. The doughy pastry would be her bedtime snack.

Finally, the clicks moved the Lisbon train to the All Aboard status. Leah rushed to the escalator that led to the lower level tracks. She pulled two suitcases behind her and stopped briefly to lift the smaller bag on top of the larger one. It contained her laptop and travel brochures collected during interviews in Madrid. She'd been in Spain for six days.

The trip to Lisbon, however, was deeply emotional for her. She'd meet Miguel there after his solo trip in the Portuguese countryside ended in that city. They'd stay for four days and return to the States together. After their Newark Airport encounter, they continued with lengthy and sexy phone conversations, always ending in a desire to be together.

"Oh, I love talking to you," he'd say. "We're spirits, my dear. It's not just my sexual attraction to you. If I ever become impotent someday, will you still talk to me?"

"Why wouldn't I talk to you?"

"Oh I don't know why I said that. What I do know is that we're not like some husbands and wives or boyfriends and girlfriends who saturate one another daily."

The longer they talked by phone without the distraction of lovemaking, the better Leah understood Miguel. His soothing voice said he loved her – but it didn't say he'd leave Susan. Leah didn't ask him to do that either. Something held her back. Her life experiences and those of other women told her men rejected pressure to leave one woman for another.

"Your cabin is in this section," said the uniformed woman with the Portuguese accent, as she checked Leah's ticket and pointed to the car behind her.

A slight hiss escaped from beneath the train creating an imaginary lift to carry her aboard and into the narrow cabin. Crisp, white sheets were tucked tightly under the narrow mattress and two puffy pillows rested against the cabin wall. A recessed cubicle was beside the bed with a glass holder. A tiny washbasin was set in a corner beside the window. Leah acclimated easily to new surroundings and quickly created a nine-hour home.

When the train pulled away from the station, she slid open

the heavy, maroon curtain that covered the window. Madrid's tall apartment buildings passed by, first slowly. They whizzed away as the train's speed increased. Her reflection in the window remained steady. It was now years older than the reflection that first appeared on a *Lusitania* window when she traveled to meet Javier in Lisbon during his business trips. The image confirmed years of repeated behavior with men: romantic interludes with fleeting intimacy versus a lifetime commitment and daily routine. Wasn't it supposed to stop when she walked out on Javier? Was Miguel a watered-down version of him? *This is the last time I'll meet Miguel anywhere as long as he lives with a woman.* The same mantra droned on in her head as she stared at herself in the window, hoping to see a nod in agreement. She didn't.

When industrial landscapes replaced city views, she closed the pleated curtains and overlapped the edges to keep out any light. During the night, the train would pass through the Extremadura countryside where bulls slept in the fields and the sunflowers had closed.

She lay in the narrow bed with her body jiggling as the train moved along the rails. Her mind replayed her latest dinner in Madrid with Rocío. This time they ate at the popular and noisy Casa Mingo, a restaurant known for its roasted chicken served family-style since 1888. Hordes of customers normally lined up outside but Leah and her friend escaped the rush on a late Sunday afternoon. The menu followed a northern-Spanish tradition from the province of Asturias where roasted chicken dishes were served with a bottle of *sidra*, Cabrales cheese and a mixed salad. Leah expected Rocío to discuss Miguel.

"Why are you meeting him in Lisbon? This dalliance was supposed to be winding down. Remember?"

"Because I can't help myself. Remember? I'm crazy about him. Maybe I love him. Maybe I don't. Can't you understand me by now?"

"I see a character flaw in you, Leah. You choose men with deep personal issues. Supposedly, your past behavior was changing, or so you told me, when you confronted Javier. This Miguel lover is living with a woman. Have you forgotten that important fact?"

"But they're not married or engaged. She only lives with him. He wants to be free. Give him time. He's in deep with shared expenses, a devalued house and job problems. Stuff like that. When we're older, it's not so easy to just up and leave. Plus, I live in New York, hundreds of miles away."

"But he's doing nothing to free himself except talk about it. Careful, my friend, I think he's using you at a deep level. He's a Casanova. It's an old description but still in style."

"I'm a big girl, Rocío. I can take care of myself. One more time with him and that's it. Wouldn't you go to Lisbon to meet a wonderful lover? Come on now, tell me the truth."

"It's been a long time since I've thought about a lover. If I did, he'd be available full time. And, please, don't call me crying about Miguel."

~ ♡ ~

The quick rap on Leah's cabin door startled her awake. The dawn created an outline around the curtains when she rose quickly to splash water on her face. The train was due at Lisbon's Santa Apolónia Station several hours before Miguel would arrive at the hotel. Now that seeing him again was a reality, exactly how did she feel? Had their attraction survived the long absence? And their bed, the undeniable litmus test of emotional entanglement, was the larger mystery. Just what would happen to them in Portugal? And hadn't she been in the situation before, running off to meet a man for a romantic interlude in a foreign country? Yes. But hope always sprang eternal with her.

"Have you been to Portugal?" he asked during a call when she revealed she'd be in neighboring Spain in a few months.

"Many times."

"Will you meet me in Lisbon?" he asked her haltingly. "I'll be there after my eight days in the countryside."

To rendezvous with Miguel again tempted her deeply. Could she do it to herself again? She didn't have to consider his offer for long because he quickly backed out of the invite.

"I simply can't do this," he said with his next call. "I'm in deep mental pain. I can't live with myself. It was one thing to run away together in Spain after our happenstance airplane meeting, but to preplan a trip with you is deceit by design. How can I look at Susan knowing I've *planned* to meet you? What's in it for you, Leah?" he asked.

"I should ask myself that question, not you."

"And what happens when we return home?"

She couldn't answer.

"I'll call you tomorrow," he said with a chill and ended their conversation.

Knowing he wouldn't call, Leah deleted his phone number, yet again. He created repeated and deepening angst.

Two weeks later, Miguel sent Leah the long overdue photo album of their trip in Spain and several promised books. His letter confessed to not having what it took to preplan a trip with her. It had to be a twist of fate if they met; yet he included specific dates and his Lisbon hotel address. To sweeten the temptation, he said he'd love to see her. But, if not, just knowing her had been an extraordinary experience.

"Why did you send me your Lisbon details?" Leah asked when she called him. The photo album rested on her lap with his face looking up at her. His looks had faded in her mind's eye, replaced by his voice.

"Because I enjoy being with you. I enjoy talking to you. I enjoy making love to you. What happened to us was authentic."

"It was authentic. I want to meet you, too. I'm so not into a clandestine rendezvous. But for you, I'll make the one exception."

What's in it for you, Leah? Miguel's pointed question replayed in her mind as she packed in the same Madrid apartment where she had packed to meet him in Salamanca a year ago. She knew they loved one another. But was that compelling enough? They lacked *authentic* life experiences to take their love to a deeper level. Could she muster up the spirit for another tryst and then walk away? One full year of this man, Leah scolded herself. Was he her catnip or was he the cat? "What's in it for me?" she said aloud and slammed her suitcase shut. "Joy. Plain and simple joy. Nothing else. That's what." Massaging the question made no sense. Life is remarkably simple when people listen to their hearts.

When the *Lusitania* arrived at Santa Apolónia Station, a warm sea breeze lifted off the nearby Tagus River. Leah hailed a cab and handed the driver a small computer printout map. An unmistakable red circle marked the hilltop boutique hotel in the Alfama district where Miguel had reserved their room. The winding drive up the narrow road was barely wide enough for two passing cars, as the cab's tires gripped the cobblestone street. Centuries-old buildings were decorated with Portugal's renowned blue-and-white ceramic tiles or painted stark white with canary-yellow trim. All had rounded red tile roofs. And as in past visits, she inhaled the unmistakable aroma of fresh sardines cooking on an outdoor grill.

The stucco façade of the tiny Hotel Alfama was an orange-sherbet color. Two tall, narrow dark-green wooden doors opened into a small reception area with red-leather furniture and glass-topped tables. Original modern art and landscape paintings hung on the walls. Their room wasn't ready so Leah sat at an opened lobby window, grateful for a wireless connection. Miguel's arrival was hours away, long enough to wonder if this short visit, a year after their Spain odyssey, could recapture the bliss. She didn't think so but noticed that the wetness in her panties said otherwise.

"Last name is Santiago," said the man with the smoky baritone to the hotel clerk, as he dropped his leather suitcase on the floor and handed over his passport.

Leah couldn't speak his name when she saw him. Instead, she walked toward him, inhaling his presence. Her movement caught his eye. He seemed to catch his breath as an ear-to-ear grin spread over his handsome tanned face when he recognized her. Instinctively, he outstretched his arms and waited for her to fill them.

"Leah, oh my beautiful Leah. It's wonderful to see you," he said and held her in a deep embrace.

"Later," she said pulling away, embarrassed as the hotel clerk stared at them. When Miguel filled out the registration form, she sized him up. He'd aged. The lines around his eyes had deepened and more gray hair curled around on his shirt collar. Maybe she looked older too.

"Take my hand," Miguel said as the clerk led them down a small metal staircase and through a narrow corridor. Sunlight streamed through a glass atrium ceiling.

When the clerk left the room, Miguel and Leah stared at the spectacular view of Lisbon. All six, extra-wide windows covered most of its outside wall. Below were ribbons of stone houses with multiple levels of winding stone staircases. In the distance, the Ponte 25 de Abril stretched across the Tagus River connecting Lisbon with Almada. The massive suspension bridge held a six-lane highway on the top level and two train tracks below. If nothing else, the lovebirds could enjoy the view for four days. Eager to make love, it took all of ten seconds for Miguel and Leah to embrace feverishly and undress each other.

"Go slow with me, please," she exhaled as he pulled her against him on their latest bed. When he rolled onto her, they melded into one another's arms, body and soul.

After their exquisite lovemaking, they lay in bed for several hours caressing each other's body; napping; kissing and making more love until they were famished for food instead of one another. They dressed, left the hotel and rode a tram into the city center. First stop was a seafood restaurant beside the Santa Justa Elevator. The Eiffel Tower-like landmark overlooked Lisbon so they rode to its top for a glass of port, sipping slowly and listening to a *fado* singer.

"I bought Portuguese wine from the countryside just for us," Miguel said. "Let's have a nightcap in bed. Talking with you at my side excites and pleases me."

"I'm game."

Returning to their hotel room, they discussed the latest books they'd read; their careers; her family and writing projects.

Miguel unexpectedly brought up Susan. Leah hadn't expected her to be along on this trip too.

"She expects me to marry her soon," he said.

"Look," Leah sighed with exasperation; she didn't want to counsel him about his girlfriend. "She's probably embarrassed by now that you haven't married her. I guarantee you she'll stop asking when people stop asking her. Hey, at least she has hope." She told him many women suffer from fear of abandonment. They stay in a bad marriage or date and live with the wrong man because they can't face living alone. Their childhood fairy tales begin with Prince Charming rescuing distressed damsels. Women carry the fantasy well into adulthood.

"I'm sorry," he said and lowered his head. "I won't mention her again."

The next morning, Miguel and Leah held hands and walked down the steep narrow sidewalk outside their hotel into the center of Lisbon. They couldn't have been happier; he with his guidebook tucked into a pocket and Leah with her curiosity turned on. They bought a bag of roasted chestnuts and shared a sweet kiss. A chirping canary in a wicker cage hung overhead. The sound was a harbinger of renewal and peace for Leah. It accompanied their steps under the orange trees as they reached the bottom of the hill.

"It's simply wonderful to be walking with you again," Miguel said.

"Did you ever think about making it permanent?" she asked and touched his heart with her fingertips.

"Sometimes."

They didn't have much Lisbon discovery time so they concentrated on seeing as many *azulejos* as possible. The colorful, hand-painted tiles were Portugal's national treasures.

They adorned homes, buildings, palaces, churches and even subway stations. Dating from the fifteenth century, the blue-and-white or multi-colored tiles recreated the country's artistic provenance from the Renaissance to present day. Lifelike figures were depicted with whimsical smiles, grandiose battles, cloud-puffed skies, galloping stallions, overflowing floral vases, mustached peasants, bountiful catches from the sea and the tile makers' fantasies.

Miguel and Leah went to the Museu Nacional do Azulejo housed in a Renaissance cloister dating from the Manueline era. He opened his guidebook, leaned slightly against her, ran his finger over the text and read the description for the seventy-five-foot-long, blue-and-white tile panorama. It depicted a Lisbon of sailing vessels and the royal palace before the 1755 earthquake. Next, he led her to the yellow carpet tiles that imitated Moorish rugs. Their visit ended in the museum's café with its eighteenth-century, hunting-scene tiles, originally from the kitchen wall of a palace. They reminded Leah of her long relationship with Javier. He was a hunter. It troubled her that she'd begun another loose affair, this time with Miguel. She wasn't supposed to do that. Her new life's purpose was to find a man who'd be her partner for life.

"You're quiet, Leah. Anything wrong?" Miguel asked.

"No. I'm fine. Simply drained from our long walk. I'm fine."

"Here, take a bite. I haven't met a Portuguese pastry I didn't like. This is sugar energy for my sugar," he said and passed his fork with a dangling *pastéis de nata* portion.

"Delicious," she said licking her lips. "Now come with me to my favorite Portuguese landmark. We need to get walking again."

They reached the Monument to the Discoveries in

the Belém district. A huge world map made of decorative stones surrounded it and traced the routes of the Portuguese navigators.

"I identify with this monument," she said and admired its prow carved with the likeness of the country's navigators who had explored the new world.

"Civilization needs explorers," Miguel said. "Otherwise, no one would venture into foreign territory. Can you imagine the living conditions they endured and the thrill of arriving at a new destination? Are we cowards compared to these great explorers?"

"I don't think so," she said. "The human spirit is the same throughout the centuries. Either one ventures into the unknown full of bravado and hope, or not. I'm an explorer. That I'm sure of. I could have stayed in my small hometown, doling out my daily life of despair as an improvised single mother. I could have simply read novels with exciting heroes, but I would have festered with jealousy because I didn't have the courage to be one. Or jealousy could have consumed me as I watched others attain more than me while I made sure my borderline gossip polluted their success. But I didn't. I bit off a huge chunk of risk and left my shackles behind. I set sail much like these explorers. And, like them, the obstacles led to realizing my dreams. Maybe that's why I love this monument and always visit it when I'm in Lisbon. What about you Miguel? Do you take the line of least resistance and wait for others to reveal an opportunity, or do you set sail on your own, eager to explore?"

While she spoke, Miguel slid his sunglasses to the top of his head so he could look into her magnificent and translucent green eyes that had left his to focus on the horizon. The sea breeze had picked up and tousled her hair, whipping it back and forth across her cheeks, which she tried to control with her slender fingers. A faint outline of her shapely legs formed as the same breeze tangled the folds of her long white skirt. Miguel wanted to be that breeze with all its force so he could place his body next to hers. He wanted to experience those legs wrapped around him. But it was Leah's mouth that captivated him. Her lips still held a slight blush of the red lipstick she'd applied that morning. With her gaze fixed on the sea highlighted by a few white caps, she gently followed the curve of her lips with the tip of her moistened tongue. Miguel longed to be her lips at that precise moment. He knew the sensation of her tongue and its steady, gentle caress along his body, stopping to take parts of it into her sensual mouth.

Right then with nature's simplistic beauty engulfing him in a capsule of immeasurable desire, he wanted nothing more than to kneel before her, bury his head in her groin and surrender for a lifetime. He knew it was a moment to declare his unconditional love, but he didn't.

"So, what's your answer, Miguel?" she asked and returned her faraway look to his dreamy eyes. "Are you an explorer ready to set sail with me into the unknown or are you only a casual armchair traveler with guidebooks written by someone else?"

"Now you're getting poetic on me. These are heady and deep questions. Come on now," he said and reached for her hand, "we've got more sightseeing before our Lisbon sun sets."

Leah paused before taking his hand. She wanted his heartfelt answer but accepted he couldn't reach a truth about them or himself, at least not at that perfect moment. "Okay. Let's sightsee. We do travel well together," she said as they left the Monument to the Discoveries. She knew a part of their souls remained on its tiled promenade for the other tourists to walk over.

By late afternoon, they trekked back up the hills to their boutique hotel. They were exhausted and Leah's calf muscles were stretched to the point of pain. Their temporary home was in the Alfama district, the historical heartbeat of Lisbon. Each corner had tiny squares with hidden shops and cafes tucked into the alleyways. Leah adored seeing the freshly washed laundry that stretched from one high apartment window across to the next. Clothes hung in perfect alignment from the smallest sock to the longest, white sheet. At the top of their street was St. George's Castle. She envisioned many fair maidens from centuries past climbing the same route.

Back on their bed for the second day in Lisbon, Miguel and Leah simultaneously reached for one another. A cat howled beneath their windows while distant bells from the nearby Igreja de Santo António de Lisboa chimed the hour. Ironically, Lisbon's patron saint was revered as a matchmaker and the protector of brides. Although Leah's wedding was decades old, she could have used his protection. She and Miguel had become insatiably addicted to their lovemaking. But they began to perish as lovers that afternoon. They couldn't continue without a greater truth to their existence. They lived miles apart with divergent lifestyles, and Miguel only wanted Leah on his time, not hers.

"*Stupendo*, Leah. It was beautiful," he said when their lovemaking subsided.

"Why am I crying?"

"After coitus, there's sadness," he said translating a Latin quote. "You're not crying, you're weeping."

On their third day in Lisbon, Miguel was laden with Susan-guilt. She was home trusting him implicitly. He became moody and detached. His character changed, something Leah saw in Spain when he faced his inner truth. He became Mike. At day's end as they climbed the steep hill to their hotel, he slowed their steps and sought refuge at an outside terrace. He ordered a drink, followed by another. Leah sipped a Coke. She sensed a showdown.

"I can't do this again. I can't meet you anywhere. I can't do this to Susan. You should be with someone who lives in New York. A man with cash. Someone with children. You can travel together."

"Your guilt has nothing to do with me finding someone else," she said. "What a stupid conclusion to draw. It's about living a life of deceit and lies. I'm not the liar. You lie to yourself most of all," she said wanting to stand on the chair and scream into the beautiful view below them. *What an idiot I am. Rocío is right. He's a charming Casanova about to dump me.* "You wanted to know what would happen when we returned to the States. Remember that?" Leah said. She wasn't about to admit she'd been a colossal jerk or that he'd used her again. Miguel moved forward in his seat anticipating her response.

"Nothing. I plan to do *nothing* when we return. You figure this out without me."

Miguel sipped his drink and began to people watch.

"You know, I'm happy we're leaving Lisbon tomorrow," she said and riveted her gaze directly into his eyes. "I bet you're a real bastard to live with when life isn't going just right for you. You use your dual Miguel and Mike personalities to fit the scenario."

"Lay off, Leah. I can't be with you and I can't be without you. Don't you see that? You're in my heart. No matter what I think, do or say to myself, you're permanently there."

"It's not *always* about you. How do you think I feel sitting in this glorious city with you pissed off because it finally dawns on you that you're cheating on Susan. You should have thought of that when you asked me to join you."

"By any chance, did you pack *Everyman,* the novel by Philip Roth? I want to read you a few pages so you'll understand how it troubles me to deceive her," he said when they returned to their hotel room.

She did have the book he'd sent her, and handed it to him. While he looked for the passage, Leah sat upright on their bed, partially dressed, with her back against the headboard. He sat beside a small table and cradled the book in his hands, like a priest about to deliver a sermon. He leaned back in the chair, stretched his legs and sighed deeply before reading the first word. Leah pulled the bed covers over her drawn knees and stared at him.

The main character, a man in his early fifties, has had his latest affair discovered by his loving wife. It humiliates her. She eloquently neuters him with her words, telling him that lying is his cheap, contemptible control over her. He's witnessing her self-inflicted humiliation caused by the incomplete information he gave her during his affairs, which he had always denied.

When Miguel read the powerful discourse between the couple, he paused at certain words to look at Leah and wince. He was a man in deep pain. An unmarried man who'd committed a searing betrayal, not only with Leah, but because of her. He was a man caught in the dilemma of how to be true to himself. For a brief moment, Leah blocked out his voice, ever so thankful she was an honest, single woman with freedom.

"I don't have any baggage at this stage of my life," she'd told him during their ugly terrace conversation. "It's all packed. I don't lie about who and what I am," adding that courage was all anyone needed to live their truth.

When Miguel paused to turn the page for more of the couple's conversation, Leah was fuming.

"Enough! Don't read any more," she hissed and stifled a scream. "Do your *mea culpa* at home. Pull your chair up in front of Susan and confess. Don't do it in front of me. Tell her we met on a plane to Spain last year and ran off as lovers. Tell her you've called me ever since. Tell her that! And be sure to add how you daydreamed about us being together in Lisbon and make sure you describe our lovemaking," she seethed. "How dare you go through a guilt trip with me. You bastard. Do it alone or do it at home."

After what had happened on their bed, what they'd experienced together and said throughout the year, how could he think she'd want to hear what he'd just read? Her throat tightened. She felt tears welling but she refused to weep, or cry, in front of him. "You wanted to know what's in it for me? Joy. This is a gift from life, Miguel. Savor it."

She left their bed and walked over to him, partially naked. His body pushed back against the chair. She grabbed the book and flung it across the room where it landed on the windowsill. A strong wind ruffled the pages sending it spiraling to the street below. Miguel looked paralyzed with fear.

"Get out of this room. Go back to that terrace, have a few drinks and leave me alone," she said and pointed to the door.

He got up quickly, reached for his wallet and left. Hours passed until she heard the key in the door. Miguel tiptoed into the room. Leah turned on the light.

"I'm really sorry," he said. "We leave tomorrow. I don't want tonight to spoil our trip. Please get up. Let's talk. I love you, but I don't know what to do. I know I say that all the time. I'm a coward."

"Yes you are," she said and joined him at their small table. He poured two glasses of wine. Their tone returned to civility. "Why do you stay with Susan?" Leah knew it was a direct-hit question.

"What could I say to her about leaving? I'm bored now and want to live alone? I made a mistake. I'm not the couple type. So many other people are involved with our decision to live together."

"Yes, you're entitled to those words. It's your life. Maybe you could tell her about me. How about that one?"

"I almost told her three times about you but never did. I'll destroy her. She loves our home. She loves me."

"But not enough? No matter how much a woman loves you, it's not enough. Right Miguel?" Leah said as she reached over to turn off the small table lamp. She couldn't soften the meaning of his words or the exasperation in her heart. When the moon disappeared behind the clouds, they sat in shadow. The metaphor was perfect.

They didn't make love when they went to bed. Leah felt like road kill lying beside him. She felt his withdrawal that morning. Normally, they'd hold hands but he had dropped hers several times throughout the day. During one conversation, she compared how they approached their lives and their lovemaking.

"I can reach intimacy quickly," she said. "But I can't commit. Seems to me you commit easily but can't reach intimacy."

"What's intimacy?" he asked.

On departure day, they boarded their flight to the States and were the only occupants in the four-seat row. Leah knew Miguel wanted her to sit beside him, which she did. After all, seatmates were what they did best. He smiled as she buckled in, knowing the game she played with herself. If the belt fit, she assumed the previous passenger was her body size. If she had to extend it, she didn't like that. If it needed tightening, she felt svelte, which she wasn't. Once aloft, Miguel settled in to read and Leah closed her eyes to remember their Lisbon bed the previous night. His arms had stayed under his pillow with his face slightly hidden.

"Don't invite me to New York unless I live alone," he said with a muffled voice.

"I won't."

Halfway across the Atlantic, he waited for her to close her book before he spoke. "I'll find a way to come to New York in a few months. I'll take a language course or something like that," he said softly.

She looked at him through squinted and confused eyes. She mentally prepared several answers: forget it, or get a grip on life or stay home with Susan. "New York has your name all over it. Sure you can visit me," she said and promised herself not to become a victim of his whimsy. She'd brush him off later. Why ruin a good flight home with an argument?

It was a golden fall day with Newark Airport approaching outside their window. Leah felt no sadness when they touched down. She wanted to go home. She wanted to be alone. She wanted to return to her center. Obviously, she lost control when Miguel came around.

"Well this is it," he said resignedly as they hugged and kissed at the dividing rope.

"Yup, this is it," Leah repeated when she drew back from his kiss. She shrugged her shoulders, turned away and walked toward the bus stop. A few steps away and almost as if she were lassoed, her head snapped back to look at Miguel one last time. He walked slowly, pulling his luggage behind him as other passengers hurried past. His face had a painful expression when their eyes met.

"I love you," he mouthed slowly so she'd understand each unspoken word.

"I love you, too," she mouthed back and continued on.

CHAPTER NINE

JUST BEFORE CHRISTMAS, Leah and her friend Maggie planned a holiday dinner. The restaurants were too crowded so they settled on Leah's place. That night, countless windows in nearby apartments brightened with holiday lights, as did a distant skyscraper with its upper spire changing colors. Maggie, middle-aged and single, was a successful actor and a hoot. Her stories always carried a theatrical flair with perfect timing for the comedic lines.

"I made love the other night," she said and winked at Leah.

"Well, aren't you the lucky one. With who?"

"No one special. Just an old friend. The plan was dinner at my place to catch up. We ended up in bed before he went home. Not a big deal. At least my legs can open again," she said hollowing with laughter. Maggie had had two hip replacements and worried endlessly before the operation if she'd ever make love again.

"They opened? Experiment or not, nothing beats a good roll in the hay. Use it or lose it, honey."

"So what's up with this Miguel guy? By the way, I finally finished *Miguel's Abduction*. Great read. Sorry it took so long but I've been in rehearsals for back-to-back shows. That means memorizing three pages of script a day. No time for other reading. Still seeing him?"

Leah corrected her. She wasn't *seeing* Miguel, like on a regular basis, but they had a four-day rendezvous in Portugal several months ago. She'd decided their affair couldn't continue. "He needs to move on with Susan at his side," she said. But she didn't want to ruin their festive night with a sad tale. "Let's forget Miguel. *Mangia.* I've cooked a divine filet mignon."

The red wine was corked and a reindeer-shaped holiday candle flickered at their table. The women passed the baked stuffed potatoes. Leah reached for the caramelized onions when her phone rang. She excused herself from the table to check the caller ID. If it were her book agent, she'd take it. Miguel's name illuminated the screen. She pointed to the phone in her hand.

"Hey, Maggie. It's Miguel. He doesn't usually call this late. Should I take it?"

"Answer him. I'll eavesdrop."

"Miguel. How are you?" she said cheerfully before he spoke.

His response was a deep sigh.

"Miguel?" This time her voice barely said his name.

His silence continued. Her heart pounded. Something was terribly wrong.

"I have prostate cancer. It's probably early stage based upon the preliminary tests," he finally said.

Prostate cancer! What would he do now? Stay with Susan? Marry her, after all. Retreat into a man with lost dreams and a life half-lived. Before this life-altering news, Leah had hoped he'd begin anew – yet again. Now everything would change.

"Oh my goodness, Miguel. What bad news. But I heard new treatments are very successful. My heart goes out to you."

Leah looked over at Maggie who was riveted to her seat, listening intently to the conversation since the tone had turned somber. Leah pointed to her groin and mouthed *cancer*. Maggie mouthed back *Wow*.

"I need to sit myself down soon and make a decision about Susan," he had said during a call to Leah before the diagnosis, adding he couldn't continue with his lies. He loved Leah. He didn't envision himself ever again living with another woman. He'd live alone for the rest of his life, and hoped she could accept that arrangement. But with this phone call, she knew his health concerns could dramatically change any future he'd envisioned. The stamina needed to live alone, face cancer and his potential impotency would be difficult.

"Can I see you in New York next month?" he asked, almost pathetically. It was sweet and tender Miguel. Mike had dumped her in Lisbon.

"I don't think so. Sorry to be so heartless but what's in it for me?"

"But I need to see you. Please. I can stay in a hotel, not in your place. We'll visit museums. We can explore a neighborhood. Can't we be friends?" he asked sounding like a child. "We don't have to have sex anymore."

"Of course we can be friends. But how can we be together and not go to bed? It's bad for my psyche to be sexually involved with you. You're still with Susan. You can come to New York. Millions do every year. But don't come looking for me. Let's discuss this later. I have a friend here for dinner. I'll call you after the holidays."

They said a sweet good-bye and hung up.

"That was some call," Maggie said. "What are you going to do?"

"Why should I see him? Now he's sick and running to me. For what? Suppose we go to bed again? Do you know what that does to me when he leaves? I'm not that strong anymore."

"Maybe he thinks he's at death's door. It's his last hurrah. You symbolize what love and lovemaking is all about. You should see him, Leah. We older women shouldn't be so restrictive when it comes to how we love a man or vice versa. Childbearing isn't an issue. Marriage isn't important either. To touch and be touched is what it's all about."

"But I'm done with clandestine affairs. Why have they turned into my *destiny?* What a lousy future that situation holds. I want a steady man. I want him to accompany me to Dana's wedding. It shouldn't be this hard."

"Give Miguel time," Maggie said. "He obviously wants out of the relationship with Susan but he's gotten himself in so deep. Now prostate cancer has reared its ugly head. Go for it, Leah. See him. Even in an affair, it's for better or worse."

Leah thought about Maggie's advice for several weeks, finally relenting out of deep concern about Miguel's health. She invited him to stay with her in New York. It was awkward to have said *don't come* and then offer her home and bed. Her relenting was unconditional. Okay to everything, she told him.

~ ♡ ~

"This is so weird. What are you doing here in person?" Leah said. She spoke first as they sat on her couch several weeks later. He had lived only in her memory and on her written pages.

"I almost cancelled the trip," Miguel said nervously.

But he'd already kicked off his loafers and rested his feet on her extra-long, brocade hassock. As they relaxed, the room's ambiance was alive with their mutual excitement.

"It's wonderful to be with you again, Leah," he said. "We're going to know one another for a long time." His words and insight had a mystical quality. "Will you allow me to take you to bed?" he asked.

"Yes."

At first, she was uneasy when he undressed and caressed her body in the middle of her living room. But as he fondled her breasts, she undressed him. They embraced in the nude until they couldn't endure their passion standing up. Miguel led Leah to the bedroom. He pulled the bed covers back and motioned for her to slip in beside him, which she did. It was one thing to make exquisite love in hotel rooms but quite another to have her daydreams materialize in her home. Despite the pleasure, the pain of his eventual departure from her bed and home crept in.

Morning came and a reality seeped into her turf. They were now on New York time, not a tourist's carefree days in Spain or Portugal. She couldn't continue the charade. If she didn't push for a change, he'd remain in Susan's bed and call her from his office. They'd plan another trip again, which would end with Leah in tears. It was time, yet again, for her to kill off an ill-fated and stupid affair.

As they relaxed in bed, breathing in one another's scent, she readied herself for the inevitable. "Okay, Miguel. Brace yourself. I need a solid answer. What's up with Susan? I can't continue if you live with her."

"I'm so bored. She's a wonderful person, but I'm so bored with her," he repeated and grimaced. "But I don't know if I can take another break up," he admitted. His chest deflated with a loud exhale. "I'm going into an experimental cancer treatment in a few weeks. Obviously, I can't leave now. I've reconciled to leaving the myth of eternal love behind. I don't have what it takes to be in an intimate, committed relationship. It pains me to admit it, but the truth about me is easier to say than to live my lies with women."

"Well. At least it's an answer. Not the one I wanted but your path is clear to me. I wish you Godspeed with your health, Miguel. We can't be together anymore. There's love here but not enough from you to sustain me." *How could I have been so stupid to keep hanging on for so long? Rocío was right.*

Leah was devastated. He was supposed to be a side dish in Spain, an unexpected and delicious pleasure, not someone sneaking into her home in the States. She wanted him to complement her life – publicly. She'd concluded he wanted freedom from his public life. But he couldn't get out. *Atado* the Spaniards called it. Bound up. He was initially trapped by his own thought process and now the ultimate entanglement, his health.

Before she could say anything else, his cell phone rang sounding like missiles aimed at their ears. He got up from their bed and reached for the phone. He looked at the number and then at Leah. They knew it was Susan. He didn't answer. Instead, he sent her to voice mail.

"Okay, okay," he said in exasperation. "I won't call you until I live alone."

"Good idea. Sorry it's ending this way. But I'm done."

"I'll go to a hotel now. I won't bother you anymore," he said, dressed quickly and left.

The next day, Leah went online and bought a train ticket to Rhode Island. Dana's wedding plans still needed attention. While she showered, Miguel called and left a wrenching message, a man grieving a loss.

"This feels so adolescent. I can't believe you're that much in love and we can't be friends. Call me back if you want to talk about it. Please."

Leah replayed the message several times. What to do? She wasn't sure about being in love any more. She was now in deep pain. Her train to Providence departed within the hour. But her compassion for Miguel and the turmoil in his life overcame reason. She dialed his number.

"I suffer when we're not getting along. I'm lost without you," he said when they met on a corner. "Let's walk."

Perhaps it was the familiar unison of their steps that prompted her to slip her arm into his as they strolled along a New York street. When he drew his elbow closer and her breast rubbed against his upper arm, an erotic feeling overcame her as naturally as saying his name. And when his free hand emphasized a point in mid-air, it stroked the afternoon hue ever so softly. That gesture was similar to the caress of his hand on her cheek whenever they met. Unlike their former emotional routes, this journey wasn't mapped. Miguel owned the conversation that day. Her words were measured.

They moved forward on the sidewalk as their stride kept its cadence. She wanted to walk backward in time regardless of the landmines. She hated being inched into another potential beginning with him that her imagination would create. She could handle what happened with him: the lies, the ecstasy, the turbulence, the Mount Everest joys and the debilitating rejection. That script was written with a pen that leaked tears and glowed with euphoria.

She found herself staring at his pant cuffs, and eventually moved her glance to his thighs. His pants enclosed his essence, the essence she yearned for. Memories of Spain and Portugal flooded with pulsating images of her legs wrapped around his creating a flash of temporary completion in her.

"Let's do something different. No museums today. How about we walk over the Brooklyn Bridge into Lower Manhattan?" she asked hesitantly.

"In March? Don't you think it's a little cold for that?"

"Come on," she urged. "The walk is incredible with drop-dead gorgeous city views. I'll hold your hand and warm you up. Ready?"

"This is what I love about you, Leah. Your spontaneity is infectious. Let's go."

They took a subway, got off at the first stop in Brooklyn and walked to the bridge in minutes. The wide, wood-plank pedestrian walkway stretched across the East River and over the traffic lanes below. With their first step, Leah was Dorothy embarking on the Yellow Brick Road with her cowardly lion. A brisk wind flapped the lapels of their jackets, tapping out a rhythmic beat. She slipped her arm through his and cuddled close as they walked.

"Were you here for 9/11?" he asked when she pointed out where the World Trade Center buildings once stood.

"No. I was researching a travel article in South America. New Yorkers have never fully recovered. We just picked up and shouldered on. Nothing stops our spirit. Plus, we have The Daffodil Project for hope and renewal."

"What's that?"

"After 9/11, millions of daffodil bulbs were given to the City through the generosity of a Dutch supplier. They were planted in parks, playgrounds, schools, community gardens and patches of green space. The following spring their brilliant yellow blooms popped up everywhere to warm the hearts of

New Yorkers and their visitors with the symbol of hope."

"That's beautiful, Leah. I admire tenacity and strength. New Yorkers have both. You're one of the city's best examples."

They were not alone on the bridge as scores of people traveled in both directions. Some rode bikes; others strolled while some jogged so fast Leah and Miguel could hear their heavy breathing. In the middle of the bridge, she touched his arm and motioned for them to look at the large ocean liner passing below and blasting its horn.

"Ever been on a cruise?" she asked.

"Once. Susan and I were with friends. Cruises are for newlyweds or the nearly dead. I prefer my European trips."

As the ship sailed farther down the river, Leah turned to Miguel and kissed him. His tongue moved cautiously in her mouth before he broke away and buried his head in her neck where she felt the warmth of his breath.

"Dance with me," she said.

"Here?"

"Here."

"You're delightfully crazy, Leah. Normally, I'd dance with you in the middle of the Brooklyn Bridge because I do it with everybody but today there's no music."

"I'll sing for you," she said and curtseyed.

Her playfulness was infectious and Miguel bowed back. He opened his arms wide and gestured for her to step into them. He put one hand behind her back, outstretched the other and pulled her close when she rested against his body.

"Start the music," he said and winked at her.

As they danced, Leah sang *Besame Mucho* to him, and a small group of passersby watched the lovers who were oblivious to their audience. When Leah finished her serenade and Miguel brushed her lips with a kiss, the crowd broke into instantaneous applause.

"Bravo," said an older man who'd stopped to watch. "Long live romance. You two are beautiful to watch."

Leah and Miguel bowed, giggled like teenagers and finished their bridge walk into Chinatown for a quick dinner.

"What would happen if I left Susan and began a relationship with you?" he asked at their table.

"My response never wavers," she said. "You'd live in Virginia – alone. I'd visit you for long weekends or longer. You'd see me in New York. Maybe we'd travel together, or alone. We'd have an open relationship – an erotic friendship – the envy of everyone. Maybe we'll live in separate apartments in the same city. Who knows?" Miguel nodded as she spoke but remained silent.

Leaving the restaurant, they walked along Canal Street toward the subway station. But before descending its staircase, he stopped her to reminisce about his deceased mother, a woman whom he adored. "I promised my mother when she was dying I'd do the three things in life she asked of me," he said wistfully.

"And they are?"

"To walk, to read and to love, but the loving part gets confusing for me."

"So I see. Work through the *process*. Remember we talked about that in Salamanca? The result is finally finding, accepting and loving one woman, not a crowd of singles."

~ ♡ ~

Back in her apartment, their conversation flowed from pop culture to favorite places to world events to their daily lives until a peaceful silence filled the room while they collected their thoughts.

"An angel's passing when it's still like this," she said to Miguel. "It's amazing. No music or distractions in this room. It's just the two of us in peaceful harmony." The small light behind his head created the perfect silhouette of her hero.

"We're the music," he said as he stretched out on her couch.

Leah sat Indian-style facing him, assuming they'd continue their talk. She wanted to revisit why he stayed with Susan. She was like a pit bull with that subject, never releasing the bone. Maybe something in their conversation would hint he was ready to leave.

He put his wine glass on the floor and looked longingly at her but her first reflex was to push back into the corner of the couch. She was hypnotized, again his obedient heroine, terrified to go to that magical planet with him. She couldn't do it to herself.

"Kiss me, Leah," he said, reaching for her.

"I want to talk about Susan again. I don't want your kisses."

"Kiss me, please," he repeated and gently placed his hand on her breast as he moved closer to her. "Why do you talk like this? You know what you mean to me. There's never been anyone like you in my life." He leaned into her opened legs. "I want you so much," he said.

And like so many times before, Miguel and Leah's bodies moved in unison. Without any coaxing, she slid down on the couch and lowered her slacks. He stood up to unbuckle his belt, lifting one leg out of his trousers and then the other. When Miguel joined her nude on the couch, she knew he'd never leave her that day or in the future.

"You'll whisper my name on your death bed," she told him.

"I have to have you now," he said.

Throughout their months of lovemaking, they had perfected a distinct rhythm. That day on the couch cushions was no different. A sweet smile crossed his face when her insides swelled to compress around his erection. Perspiration collected between her breasts. The back of her neck was drenched. There were no discernable words from her, only soft moans.

"The feeling is just like before. It never dulls," he said.

Sometimes her climax was so intense her stomach muscles were tender for several days. It was the only tangible way for him to *feel* how much she loved him. Sometimes a voice deep inside of her screamed his name and sounded light years away as they climaxed together. Other times, and for unknown reasons, she'd sob and he'd kiss the tears that streaked her cheeks. That day Miguel released a long, deep primal scream that echoed inside Leah's chest.

"Oh my God, I'm prepared to die at this moment," he said and collapsed on top of her. "I can't make love to anyone the way I make love to you. No one. Making love like this is the essence of life. You're in my heart, Leah. I'm consumed with erotic memories of you. They're permanent no matter how hard I try to erase them from my consciousness."

"Do you say that to Susan when you make love to her?" she asked and despised her jealousy.

"No," he answered with questioning eyes.

"Does she love you?"

"I'm not sure. When we make love, she says nothing. I'm not making love to her the way I did in the beginning."

"Why do you bother at all?"

"Couples have to make love sometimes. It's a matter of dignity for the other person."

"What about my dignity?" Leah asked and got up from underneath him and went to the bathroom.

His eyes followed her but he didn't speak.

As Miguel slept beside Leah that night, she lay awake and inhaled his exhale. If she moved away or moved her foot, he followed with his body. When he put his hand on her shoulder, she covered it with hers. She lay paralyzed with emotion. As for the essence of her life and her heart, she needed honesty from him, not sweet words. She wanted him in total. She wanted reality. She wanted Susan gone. She wanted him to accompany her to Dana's wedding and be her lifelong companion.

Leah awoke to the mourning doves cooing outside her window and waited for Miguel to move before she brushed her lips over his.

"Buenos dias," he said and got out of their bed. "Want some orange juice? I'll get breakfast ready and you make the bed," he continued and left the room as his words trailed behind. He'd become comfortable in her home and moved about like an animal marking his territory. When he returned from her kitchen, he held two juice glasses.

"You sang to me on the bridge. Now let me sing to you, but in Spanish," he said, clearing their breakfast dishes and returning to the dining table. "Can you understand these words? They are beautiful," he asked after finishing the first few lines.

Leah shook her head no, which prompted his translation. He said it wasn't literal but she'd get the gist of the song.

If I could say how pretty is love, you would feel about me what I feel about you. You'd dream without sleeping. You'd fly without wings and tell me you love me. "This is the best part," he continued. *Go to sleep thinking I'm thinking about you. Wake up dreaming you are living for me. Only for me. Only for me.*

Leah winked and blew him a kiss.

But as he prepared for his departure to Virginia later that morning, their dreamy moods changed. "This is tragic. There's so much I want to give to you," he said with his suitcase at her door.

"I've heard those words before. I need action," she said with a sweet smile. "I know you love New York. You can see yourself living here, but it's not reality."

He'd soon undergo weeks of radiation treatment, uncertainty about his sexual life and mounting issues in the faltering jewelry business he owned. Then there were Susan's waiting arms. New York wasn't a reality in his future as Leah imagined his life. She didn't cry when he left.

What to do about Miguel was becoming an all-consuming issue for her. She couldn't shake him. Did she love him? She wasn't sure anymore. How could she? It saddened her that he didn't know her deeply. He knew a dinner companion; someone to move beneath him in the truest form of ecstasy; a friend to call when the day's hours waned. He didn't see her with her children. Or watch her dance around her apartment when she cleaned it moving to a song on the radio. They didn't sit beside her fireplace reading the paper or listening to fine music. He couldn't experience Leah fully: her spirit, her joy, her tears and her boredom. And when she thought about his dual personalities – Miguel and Mike – she didn't truly know him either.

She was emotionally lost and needed a man's point of view. She decided to seek out Terrance Burke, a Central Park carriage driver and one of her best friends. She found him standing beside his horse, Patricia, at Grand Army Plaza, the entrance to Central Park at West 58th Street and Fifth Avenue. A mammoth, gilded bronze statue of General William Tecumseh Sherman marked the square. Leah admired Nike, the Goddess of Victory, who shared the platform with the soldier.

"Leah, darlin'. How the hell are you?" Terrance said with open arms and pulled her into a hug scented with horse smells.

He'd nicknamed the two of them "phone bitches" because they'd talk for hours, howling with laughter. They were two tuning forks that got their vibrations from one another. He knew he was her rock and counsel when she needed a guy's perspective on romance.

"Let's go for a ride," he said and reached for her hand.

They walked to his white, horse-drawn carriage with two bunches of plastic roses affixed to the frame. Terrance gave Patricia a carrot and guided Leah up the metal steps and into the carriage. A Cinderella moment for her. When his switch tapped the horse's hindquarters, the three of them bolted forward into the hectic traffic on West 58th Street.

That day Terrance wore a top hat, which formalized him. Off the carriage, his wanderlust had taken him on some of the world's best adventures. He realized in his childhood that he never wanted to marry. Instead, he traveled the globe, purposely on a shoestring. He was now in his thirty-fifth year of sleeping on the ground in small huts, or riding death-defying rapids, or scaling mountains just for an eternal thrill. The walls of his New York home displayed framed bugs he'd collected and paintings he'd completed during quiet moments. Long swords were stacked in an umbrella stand. His bookshelves held native hats, penis gourds and tiny memorabilia, all perfect touchstones for his action-packed, show-and-tell stories. A map of the world covered a bedroom wall where his eyes retraced his trips as he lay in bed, often with a girlfriend at his side.

Patricia's hooves accented their conversation while Terrance turned halfway around on his seat to talk directly to Leah.

"So how's it going with your seatmate-lover? Still doing him?"

"Can we elevate this conversation, please?"

"You're not thinking about marriage, are you? It's a hoax. The anti-fun of life. Don't go there with your vivid imagination."

"Of course not but we're falling hard for one another. But why is he still living with Susan? This is getting crazy."

"He stays in that unfulfilling relationship out of fear. Fear to be alone. Fear of rejection. Fear of change. Fear of big risks. Fear to live a life on the edge. Fear of you."

"Okay but what do I do about him in my life?"

"Keep him as a drive-by until you find the right one," he teased with a glint in his eye.

"I can't do that," she said. "He's different. Maybe he's around for a reason. It's because of him that I wrote our love story. The process unearthed a deeper level of self-love and understanding of my life as a collector of affections. But meeting him told me I want to change that approach. He's really the man of my dreams."

"That's a massive change for you. Can I meet him some day? I'll give you my honest and brutal opinion. Trust me. I *really* know guys. Maybe he's a jerk, and you don't see it. I'll protect you."

"No. You can't meet him. You know too much about me.

He's not a jerk. Stop fooling with my head. Please tell me what attracts these men to me? I'm not a raving beauty. I don't have a drop-dead-gorgeous body. I'm financially secure but I dislike picking up the dinner check. I like a home life but not constantly. It isn't only about lovemaking since my lovers stay around for a long time. I always thought there were many women just like me. Maybe not."

"All your joy and laughter happened after your divorce. You listened to your intuition. Not to someone else's. You took huge risks – divorcing and then leaving Rhode Island for a better life – that turned the risks into new opportunities. You've become fearless living your life, unlike others who are mired in misery or in half-lived lives."

"You really think that about me?"

"Absolutely, but you're scary to lots of guys. They know intuitively not to get into the trenches with you. You're a winner. If they're not, why get bloody?"

"Thanks, but I think you just insulted me. Maybe you're right. I appreciate the pick-me-up. I owe you a dinner."

"You're welcome, and I'll make sure you come through with the offer. But don't ever forget that these unfilled men you meet live a long-lost truth through you. You have magical thinking, Leah. Don't lose it. Freedom is the ultimate joy in life. Enjoy yours. If you're destined to be with Miguel, it will happen."

He then turned in his seat to tighten his grip on Patricia's reins. She'd quickened her step since their ride was almost over. When Leah left Terrance at the carriage stop, his good-bye hug was longer than usual.

A heavy sadness overcame her as she walked home. Was it her imagination or was there an unusually large number of couples holding hands? Was she alone because of her collector-of-affections approach to men? Probably yes, so she made a decision. No more entanglements with unavailable men. They'd never dictate the relationship. No more waiting for the phone to ring. No more romantic interludes. Her free lifestyle regarding men had been a fabulous run, but it was over. She'd live a celibate life. The thought of that limiting choice was daunting but the rewards outweighed the pain of a bad choice.

CHAPTER TEN

AFTER MIGUEL'S NEW YORK VISIT ENDED with broken dreams and despite Leah's resolve to keep him at bay, she still answered his phone calls. When they'd hang up, she'd promise herself to limit the calls. She'd be an occasional phone friend lending support during his cancer treatments. Several months after they ended, and one evening close to midnight, he called her from his home. Susan was away for the weekend. A CD in the background played a Spanish classical guitar.

"Oh, Leah." He sighed. "I want you beside me right now. I miss you so much. My libido returned. I'm a lucky man. Can you imagine me in your bed with you?" he asked sweetly and sent a kiss through the phone.

The following night, he called again with the Spanish classical guitar in the background.

"Hi sweetie. Just want to say I love you. You're in my thoughts. I'm trying to get away to see you in New York. Can't wait to be together again."

"Stop, Miguel," she screamed. "Stop the erotic travelogue. Stop the stupidity. Leave me alone. No more phone calls. I'm beginning to hate you. Grow up. Enough. I can't continue.

Enjoy your life with Susan. I'm done." she said. And she slammed down the phone.

He didn't call back.

Susan handled the household accounts. Was it by chance or deliberate when Miguel didn't intercept the telephone bill that showed his midnight calls to Leah? He'd planned to pay it privately. He also planned to tell Susan that their relationship was over. She was a good woman who needed to find someone else despite how much she loved him. Although she'd taken care of him through his illness, that wasn't enough to stay together. She shouldn't just be a nursemaid. He wanted to live alone. He wanted Leah in his life. Susan would be told the devastating news after the surprise birthday party her family had planned for her. Miguel had to attend. When she was sick with pneumonia, he had to care for her. But the phone bill arrived before he had a chance to tell her anything about the break-up.

Susan stood beside him in the foyer one rainy afternoon as the postman approached their home. Miguel watched as their mail slid through the door slot and landed on the floor. The phone bill was on top of the pile. How could he pick up one envelope? He couldn't. He never took care of the mail. Instead, he froze and watched Susan retrieve the envelopes and walk into the kitchen.

"Hey, honey? Did you call someone in New York?" she yelled over her shoulder a few minutes later. "Why at midnight and talk for ninety minutes? The next night you talked for five. We don't know anyone in New York. What's going on Miguel?"

Without answering, he walked into the kitchen, took her

hand and led her to a wingback chair in the living room. They'd chosen two for their new home. He sat opposite her in his chair and paused grasping for the right words. He got up and paced in front of the fireplace. Susan's eyes followed him, distressed and questioning. When he finally spoke, the mood in the room had already turned ugly.

"I met a woman on a plane to Spain several years ago. When we landed, we ran away together like fairy-tale lovers. I suffered tremendous guilt when I returned to you, determined to keep her only as a memory. I never planned this affair, Susan. You trust me implicitly when I travel alone. I tried to forget her but she haunts me. I saw her when I was in Portugal. I lied to you when I went to New York. She lives there. I didn't just visit the museums; I slept with her and loved her more. I've talked to her for over a year from my office. I love her. You and I have to part now."

He blurted out his confession in one swoop. He bowed his head and couldn't look up. A slight tremble traveled throughout his body. "You don't deserve this kind of hurt. I'm so sorry. I had plans to tell you but there was never the right moment."

Susan sat ramrod still. Her mouth dropped open, closing only to swallow away the lump in her throat. Her stare transfixed on him. "Oh, my God. How could you do this to me? We love one another. I trusted you when you traveled. Our friends questioned your solo trips, but not me. I understood your need to reconnect with your European roots. But another woman in your life? Impossible!" Deep, wrenching gasps and sobs escaped uncontrollably from her body as she doubled over in the chair. "You despicable human being. Another woman in your heart and you slept beside me night after night. Do you think of her when you make love to me?" she screeched.

Miguel went to place his hand on her shoulder but she flung it away.

"I tried so hard to be faithful. I'm a monogamous man. I've never done anything like this. I hate myself for this deceit by design. I hate my job. I hate our boring life, Susan." His chest heaved with each deep breath he took. "You deserve more than what I can give you. You're a wonderful person but living as a couple is a fraud to me. I love you more as a friend and not enough to have resisted the temptation of another woman."

"Love me?" she asked incredulously. "You love me? No, Mike, you love yourself." She never called him Miguel. "We're in our late fifties. What else remains but to enjoy one another for the rest of our lives? We can become grandparents when my children have children. I nursed you through prostate cancer. Was she on your mind as you hoped for continued erections? Would your New York whore want you if you couldn't get it up? I accepted that probability. I love you unconditionally."

"She's not a whore. I don't know what she'd accept."

"There's a Mexico trip planned for us. How can I face our married friends and lay beside you knowing there's another woman in our bed?" What she didn't add was that their friends were hoping he'd propose marriage to her.

"I'll never trust you again, never," she continued and began to pace the floor. "Why are you well into middle-age and still chasing a fulfilling relationship? Don't you remember you said I was *the one.* You bastard. Maybe one discretion is forgivable but not months of a clandestine threesome," she seethed and glared at him. "What's wrong with me, Mike? Why does our life bore you? What does this woman have that I don't? Why do this to me?" she said pathetically, in a softer voice.

How could he say she lacked everything – everything –

Leah possessed? He didn't. Instead, he saw Leah's image and knew he'd forever regret losing her if he stayed with Susan. Prostate cancer and the successful treatment had changed him. He wanted out of the lies he'd allowed to rule his life. The flame wasn't worth the candle. Leah used that phrase to describe life and how people burn theirs.

"Is she waiting for you in New York?" Susan said breaking their icy silence.

"I don't know. Maybe she's gone. I can't blame her. I'll live alone, with or without her. Lying to you is tortuous and so wrong. I became two separate men. You're a wonderful woman but…."

"You can have your wish. Live alone in this home we created," Susan said and hurled her wine glass into the fireplace.

Miguel backed up. He'd never seen such hatred toward him as she had in her eyes.

"You sleep alone in our bed. Take my name off the mailbox. I want no connection with you. Change the telephone message. You mop up," she said through muffled gasps and ran into their bedroom where she dissolved in tears on their bed. Within the hour, she grabbed the keys to her car and rushed out the door.

When Susan left, he heard the wheels of her car screech as she pulled out of their driveway onto the country road. Dusk settled as Miguel sat alone and wondered when love died. When was the precise moment, the exact hour, day, week, month or year when loving someone turned into a shrug of the shoulder? When was the dividing day? When did his eyes turn blind to Susan's naked body lying in their bed night after night after night? At what point did making love to her become routine, an obligation on Wednesday and Saturday nights? After Leah's touch, whenever Susan reached for him in their bed, he'd often stammer, mumbling something about how he didn't want to make love. Maybe later. She'd sigh into her pillow while he feigned sleep.

When did the harness of habit suffocate him? That yoke of companionship, a hold others cherished had choked him – again. He knew Susan's routine, her footsteps, her idiosyncrasies, the sigh of her climax and her menu choices. The mystery and chase had morphed into the tyranny of monogamy. He'd begun to avoid her mundane and multiple cell phone calls. He wondered why she'd stayed so long since she wanted marriage, and he didn't.

He listened to jazz and Spanish music that night. He drank heavily; an opened bottle of Carlos V brandy was nearby. He read a book in Spanish, saying the words aloud to break the silence around him. He cried deep sobs as he sat in the dark. He'd never experienced such sorrow. A part of him was dying. He was the only mourner.

During that solitude, he dissected his approach to life and his inability to return a woman's love completely. After he declared his love, which always happened at the beginning, he couldn't sustain it. It didn't feel natural. Flashbacks of all the women who had loved him over decades unraveled in his memory. He was always the object of their love, a familiar and satisfying role for him. When they were milked dry, he'd end the relationship and begin romancing, seducing and finally bedding someone new.

"You will never find another woman who'll love you as much as I do," he heard repeatedly when dumped women tried to console themselves and repair the damage of his slaughter.

Now, life had granted his wish to be alone. But it didn't prepare him for the terror and the despondency he felt. There was no one to talk to about it, either. His male friends were ensconced in relationships and content with one woman, making him an oddball. When his footsteps echoed across the bare hardwood floors and he saw guidebooks lined up for new destinations and new women to conquer, he knew it was the life of a fool. He was all bravado. A man without a center.

Leah's beautiful voice spoke to his soul during that tortuous night. *Work the process, Miguel. Instead of being the object of love, discover how to give it unconditionally. The result is finally finding, accepting and loving one woman forever, not a crowd of singles.*

When he envisioned making love to Leah again, his hand moved over the zipper on his pants. But it wasn't just the sex with her. It was all of her that consumed him. He wanted, and needed, to share his life with only her. But it was all so new, this one-woman love. Could he trust himself? Everyone had a personal truth they eventually had to acknowledge. His was to accept Leah as the only women he wanted to *give* his love to. Even if she rejected him, she'd still have it for a lifetime.

That revelation was like an illumination in his confused and broken mind. He opened his agenda book and created a To Do List. A truthful life was about to unfold; he mapped out his future with or without Leah. He wasn't very optimistic that she was still with him.

But what would he do with the family-owned jewelry business? It wasn't prospering in the recession. His brothers questioned his sloppy business style. His heart wasn't in the firm; he wasn't interested in staying in Virginia. He decided a family meeting should be planned with the company lawyer.

He'd tell everyone he couldn't live someone else's expectations of what he should be. He was relinquishing his partnership and moving away.

The freedom gained by telling Susan that they were finished and confronting his family with his departure from the business spurred him on to reach for the telephone to call Leah right away. He not only loved her; he also liked her and respected her advice about not using her as a reason for leaving Susan.

"You only leave for yourself," she'd said. "Make the decision based upon your needs and how you'll embrace a new life, with or without a woman."

Miguel left Susan for himself. If Leah weren't in his life, he'd carry on with her in his heart. But at the deepest level, he wanted her forever. As he dialed her number, a familiar tremble ran through his body. A notepad with disjointed thoughts rested on his lap, although he'd memorized them. When her cell rang four, five, six times, he hoped she didn't recognize his number and was ignoring the call.

"Hello," she said hastily.

"Leah," he said softly with his heart pounding.

"Miguel. Is that you? I can hardly hear you."

"Yes, it's me. I have something to say so please let me speak first. I hope you still want to hear these words. Susan and I are no longer together. She found out about you and me because of a phone bill. I planned to tell her sooner. She's moving out over the weekend. I'm selling my share of the business. I'm moving to Spain and New York. I was also a collector of affections until I met you. Can I see you again?"

"Oh my God, Miguel. I've wanted this conversation since our night in Segovia. Why did it take a phone bill for you to break with Susan? Would you have stayed otherwise?"

"No. Hard for you to believe, I'm sure. You know I always wanted to live alone. I still do, but my heart doesn't want to be alone. I've had so many break ups with women. I thought I'd never find the right one until you came into my life. Sometimes it takes brutal lies, like those I told to Susan and myself, to discover who we truly are. Can we make a new life together? Will you travel with me again, Leah?" he asked before she could speak. "I'm frightened about this new life but not as much if you're beside me."

"Live your life with gusto, Miguel. Take bold chances. Feel deep emotions. You're on the right path. I'll try to begin something new with you, but on our terms, not just yours," she said sweetly. "But you don't have a good track record. You cheated on Susan to be with me. Honestly, I don't trust you. But congratulations for leaving her. It was the right thing to do. Think some more. We'll talk later. I'm too busy with Dana's wedding. I need a clear head. You're too much angst for me right now, but I'm proud of you. Got to go. Dana is calling on the other line."

"Ah, wait a minute," he said. "Please don't hang up so quickly. I need a shred of hope here. Now that I've declared myself, so to speak, and I'm twirling in the breeze, do I stand a chance with you? I'll sleep easier with your answer."

"Sure you do," she said sweetly. "There's a deep love here. History, too, even if some of it was ugly. We haven't been all that kind to one another. But how could we be since we lived a lie? It was a delicious one when we were in bed or talked on the phone for hours, but the reality was you lived with and also slept beside Susan. Now you don't any more. I need to digest this change. I wanted you *accessible.* Remember? Now you are.

Let me leave you with a thought: on a scale of one to ten, you're batting nine right now. *Besos* my love. Bye for now."

After the call, Miguel remained in his leather chair listening to music. He pictured himself in bed with Leah and smiled. He knew she loved him. They'd finally be together. The vision made him euphoric and hot before he dozed off. When the doorbell rang, it jolted him awake. But it was the flashing lights on the top of a car parked in the driveway that set his heart racing. Something was wrong.

"Can I help you, officer?" Miguel said rubbing his eyes awake.

"Are you Miguel Santiago? Is this your house?"

"Yes. What's wrong?" he asked.

"There's been a serious accident involving Susan Ingram. Her license listed this address. Witnesses said she was speeding and driving erratically, like a crazy person. She sideswiped a tree. Damn lucky she didn't sever the car in half."

"What do you mean by serious accident? Is she dead?" he asked breathlessly and leaned heavily against the door.

"No. But badly beat up. She's in intensive care at St. Paul's Hospital. Are you her husband?"

"No. I'm a friend. She lived here until tonight."

"Did you have a fight?"

"More than that."

"You might want to see her. It's serious," the officer said as he returned to his car.

The guilt Miguel experienced was profound as he drove to the hospital. His lies and deception had almost killed Susan. She didn't deserve to have fallen so deeply in love with his decaying soul. She'd given their relationship her all. She really did pick up his socks; washed his laundry; cooked most nights;

treated him to dinners at their favorite restaurants; decorated their home for the holidays; arranged their social calendar; paid the bills; made passionate love to him whenever he wanted and never questioned his fidelity. In return, he lived with her and portrayed himself as her better half. Nevertheless, they weren't married, and he never wanted to be a fulltime husband. He tried so hard to make it work on the surface, but the true Miguel traveled alone to his Promised Lands, enticed a seatmate named Leah Lynch into bed – and, yes, he did have a one-night stand in Italy, just as Leah had suspected, that caused him to miss his flight home. Elena's card was in his shirt pocket when Leah surprised him at Newark Airport. He even emailed and called her in Italy from his office in Virginia. She had potential. Thinking about that lie to Leah made him sick to his stomach.

He pulled over, opened the car door and vomited onto the asphalt. He saw himself as the arrogant one in all relationships. By the time he pulled into a hospital parking space, he couldn't get out of his car. Instead, he buried his head in his hands and sobbed. He vowed to change his life from that moment on. He would never lie to another woman or to himself, ever again. But what path would his new life take?

"She's in Room 104," the nurse said when he entered the floor of the hospital.

"104?" he asked. He was dazed.

"Yes. Down the hall on your right."

The number was hauntingly familiar. It was the same room number from the Segovia hotel where he and Leah fell deeply in love and where Susan had died in his heart that night.

Entering her hospital room, he paused. An illuminated green screen beside her bed showed blips, and an IV bottle drained into her bruised arm. Her daughter had already sent a bouquet of flowers. Miguel walked hesitantly to the side of her bed, leaned over her still head, ran his hand along her hairline and kissed her forehead.

"Hey, Susan. It's me, Miguel. I'm so sorry. Get well, please."

She opened her eyes slightly, closed them and breathed deeply. A tear ran down each cheek.

He went over to a nearby chair and sat down without taking his eyes away from her until the dawn illuminated the room. So many thoughts. *Oh Susan, why did it come to this? Why does a dying love hurt so much? How can we go on now, together or apart? I'm so sorry. You don't deserve this horror I brought to you.*

"She'll be here for a few weeks and will need physical therapy. Will she go back to your home?" the attending physician asked Miguel the next morning.

"Ah. Probably." What else could he say?

Miguel visited Susan daily. She slowly regained strength but avoided any meaningful conversations with him. Her family visited as well, only speaking to him when spoken to. The couples they'd shared dinners with sat at her bedside, their scorn like an impenetrable wall between them. But he stayed in the room. It was the least he could do. He stopped at the business office and pledged to pay the bills not covered by insurance. A hospital supply company was contacted to set up the rehabilitative equipment she'd need in their home. A home-care aide was hired. He covered every aspect of Susan's full recovery except the one for her broken heart.

"Oh my God, Leah, what am I going to do?" Miguel asked when he called her several days after the accident.

"What are you talking about? What's the problem?"

"Susan left the house the night we split up. She was speeding and crashed her car into a tree. She almost died. She needs months of rehab and will return to our home."

"Do you love her? Sorry to be so blunt here, but what's at risk is your future happiness. She'll recover but will you if you stay with her?"

"No. I don't love her. I love you. What a crazy question to ask now. I'm so guilty for what I did to her. What should I do?"

"I'll be blunt again. You have to view this as an accident only. It wasn't your fault. Don't take on that kind of guilt. But do take care of her needs. Pay all the expenses. Get her back on her feet. You leave the house this time. Maybe hand over the deed. Or sell the house and financially help her find another. I don't know, Miguel. Do something positive but make it honest."

"You've got to be kidding. I can't leave her a second time. She might do this again. How cold-hearted you are. You just want me to be with you."

"I want you to be with yourself first. Then decide what woman you want permanently in your life. Go deep inside. Find your truth. Don't keep lying to Susan, me or your next women. When you avoid the truth, it hurts everyone more in the end. Man up, Miguel. What's happening now and how you handle it will set the course for the rest of your life. You're a wonderful, smart, compassionate, giving, funny and sexy man. You also want to live alone. See yourself as I see you. I'm crazy about you. Don't you know that by now? But I want you to be crazy about yourself."

CHAPTER ELEVEN

LEAH FEARED GOING TO DANA'S WEDDING from the day her daughter placed her slender hand with its stunning engagement ring in her mother's hand. The anxiety continued throughout the bridal showers and wedding plans. Returning to Providence as the mother of the bride meant reliving an unhappy and painful past, coupled with one of the most beautiful days for her family. Was she an awful mother for feeling this way?

A week before the ceremony, Leah arrived in her hometown and registered in a hotel. Before she and Dana worked on last-minute wedding arrangements, she'd stroll through the city's East Side neighborhood, several blocks away. Prosperous seventeenth- and eighteenth-century China Trade entrepreneurs had built elaborate mansions along the brick-inlaid sidewalks. By the 1950s, many of the homes became cheap rooming houses with flimsy partitions. Daytimes, the area showcased prestigious, ivy-covered Brown University. By evening, Benefit, Power, Prospect and other streets – all names associated with puritanical, Yankee families – became the pathways of fortune for prostitutes who wore feathers in their hats and glitzy earrings dangled from their lobes. They wiggled down streets once trod by Edgar Allen Poe and George Washington. They even sauntered past the First Baptist Church in America, built in 1775, still serving an active congregation.

The restoration of the East Side's "Mile of History" began when the Providence Preservation Society encouraged wealthy families to buy into the area and renovate homes, which they did, one by one. Wide floorboards now gleamed under oriental rugs that curved with the natural sag of time. A mantel embellished with a Greek key frieze held family photos. Mahogany, Hepplewhite furniture, flowered-chintz couches and starched white curtains blended to make a lovely home. Outside, flowering cherry trees shaded rows of purple and yellow pansies on sidewalks that heaved from winter frosts and age. And in the backyards, neat white picket fences enclosed tulip beds.

Leah's strolls through historical Providence helped her process her earlier life when she lived in the city. Although New York was her soul's home and her insatiable wanderlust took her to many countries, she was still a Rhode Islander. She could accept that. Returning to the street where she once lived as a married woman and mother of two children had a deeper impact.

Who she'd become compared to who she once was on that street made it difficult for her to lay claim to that former life. She was now a transformed and evolved woman, ever so grateful to be one. But she had to return to her former home. Dana wanted her mother at her side as she dressed for the wedding ceremony.

"Stop at this corner. I'll walk the rest of the way," Leah told the taxi driver when they reached Williston Avenue. She stood motionless looking at her former street, until a black-and-white soccer ball rolled by, hit the curb and then rebounded at a diagonal until it came to rest against her shoes. The young player shouted for Leah to kick it back to him but there was no reaction from her. She continued to stand in place taking stock. Her face was still but for a small private smile.

The player shouted again but still no reaction. It was as though she didn't hear. Her smile faded, like a ripple on a river. The child, exasperated and confused, ran up to her to retrieve the ball himself. But as he picked it up and was about to run back to the game, something made him stop and look at the strange woman a second time.

"Are you looking for someone?" he asked.

Moments passed with no reply from Leah but something about this smartly dressed woman held the boy's attention. It was the stillness of her face. He was startled when the mask suddenly melted, and she looked down at him and smiled the smile again.

"Me," she said in a tone both sweet and sad. "I'm looking for me. The woman who once lived here."

Sunshine filtered through the trees as she walked down the street where birds hopscotched over branches. A puff of wind juggled shriveled leaves, swirling them over cement sidewalks and property lines. Pat, the mailman, still weaved back and forth across the street, from house to house as if he were lacing a shoe with his path. Flap, flap, flap, mailboxes were filled and Pat's bouncing footsteps down the front steps prompted doors to open and close shut as the occupants retrieved their mail.

Leah would never have traded her children's years on the street where they were born. It was a place of lasting friendships for them. She still saw their Big Wheels rolling through the puddles, the block parties, the lemonade stands and the tree forts. When her former home came into view, Leah wasn't sure she could go in but she had to for Dana's sake. She rang the bell.

"Welcome home, Leah," said Sun-Hee, Jim's wife, as she extended her hand and smiled. "Welcome back is what I meant to say," she corrected herself with a giggle.

"Thank you. It's a pleasure to be here," Leah lied.

"Your daughter is waiting for you to help with her dress," said Sun-Hee and pointed to the upstairs staircase.

On the wedding day, Leah stood in her daughter's former bedroom and fastened the long line of satin buttons running up the back of Dana's wedding dress. She shed a joyful tear with each closure, as did her daughter.

"Nervous, dear daughter?"

"Not that much. I just can't wait to be Steve's wife and make you a grandmother. Hopefully, I'll be as fantastic a mother as you are."

"Honest? Do you mean those words, Dana, considering this house experienced a major catastrophe with the divorce?"

"We never would have made it to the great shape we're all in. You changed us all for the better." Dana wiped at a tear and checked her mascara in a mirror. "I'm so proud of you for what you did. Don't ever think it was a mistake. But I want you to have a steady companion, Mom. If you did, you wouldn't be alone today."

"Now, now. This day isn't about me. It's all about you and Steve. I'm fine without a man beside me. Once I get back to

New York, I'll start looking again. Your compliments about how I raised you are wonderful to hear. But come on now, let's not get all gushy. Your dress is buttoned. Put on your veil. The photographer is waiting."

At Our Lady of the Rosary Church and as Mendelssohn's "Wedding March" began, Clarke, Leah's son, offered his arm to his mother to accompany her down the church's long aisle.

"Take a deep breath and smile. You should be proud of yourself. You look beautiful, too," he said under his breath.

Several hundred people were seated at the wedding Mass, many not invited to the reception. Former classmates from Dana and Clarke's elementary school came to see the bride. Some were simply nosy voyeurs who wanted to see Leah, the woman everyone predicted would fail.

When she lived on Williston Avenue, the neighborhood women kept each other's secrets and stories of discontent. But she was the only one to divorce and leave them behind. Those same women sat halfway down the aisle. As she nodded in their direction, she pictured baby carriages, sewing classes, sharing recipes and coupons. She also saw that the light had diminished in some eyes. A deep and unmistakable boredom had settled in. Were they thinking they should have changed their lives too? Her stomach was in knots. Tears welled. Her bottom lip quivered. Clarke tightened his grip on her arm as they walked past peering eyes on both sides of the aisle.

"You're doing great, Mom. You're much better off than most of the people here," he said and kissed her check as he led her to the front pew.

The moment then belonged to Dana who'd taken her father's arm to walk proudly down the long aisle, nodding and smiling to the approving crowd. Leah expected the churchgoers to burst into applause. Jim deserved this day with his daughter. He was a good father with decent values that still worked. He'd picked up the mantle of parenthood when Leah dropped it during those dark days after the divorce. Without him, she might not be the woman she was today.

After the wedding ceremony, an informal reception line formed near the azalea bushes that were outside the church's entrance. It surprised Leah that she wanted to join it. Many guests lined up to greet her, congratulate Dana and meet Steve, her new husband.

"I've missed you so much. Welcome home," one friend said and hugged her tighter than she expected. "You did it your way. Great job," she whispered into Leah's ear before moving along in the line.

"How fortunate you are to have such a beautiful family," another friend said. "We've missed you on the street but now see where your journey took you and your children."

"I wish I had your courage," said the woman who once confided in Leah that she loved a man who wasn't her husband. Their affair was decades old, but she didn't have what it took to leave her doomed marriage. Her face was etched with drawn lines, made more noticeable by eyes that no longer held a glow.

Slowly, with each hug, whisper of approval or a certain warm smile, the demons in Leah's mind about her ugly past faded until, one by one, they disintegrated in the bright sunlight. Everyone had moved along with his or her life, lives that still included Leah as a friend. Only she still relived vivid memories of *her former self* that no one wanted to recognize any more.

After months of unnecessary angst about Dana's wedding, simply standing in a reception line where others forgave or embraced her for who she was had an overwhelming and freeing effect on Leah. If only she had a special man to share her joy. Telling her New York friends about this transforming moment wouldn't have the same impact. She wanted someone beside her right then as she basked in her own glory and forgave herself.

"Who's that man, Mom? He keeps looking at us. I don't know him from the neighborhood, work or anywhere else. Do you?" Dana said turning her head toward the sidewalk across the street.

Leah looked in that direction. The handsome man's face was one she'd kissed many times. She knew his wide grin very well; it had smiled at her often. He was no stranger. Miguel Santiago was standing there in his finest suit staring at her. He was the only person she wanted at her side that day, but she'd given up hope they'd have a future together. Maybe she was wrong.

"My eyes hurt when they don't see you," he said when Leah approached him. "I love you deeply. That's why I'm here. As for Susan, I took your advice. She's well cared for now. We parted amicably. Leah, can we spend the rest of our measured lives together? Please say yes. I have two tickets to Spain in my pocket. One is for you," he said hurriedly when he hugged her and buried his face in her neck. A slight tremor went through his body to match the one she was having.

"Of course I'll go to Spain with you. There's a life waiting for us in New York if you want," she answered. But she felt a slight hesitation for having said yes. She looked into Miguel's eyes, deeper than she'd ever done. A profound silence hung over them. Were they capable of relinquishing *their former selves?* Had they really changed? Had they completed the process to alter their lives permanently to be with only one person to love unconditionally? Yes. She'd believe in them, yet again. She'd trust he was ready for a deeper intimacy with only her. The alternative of not being together wasn't acceptable anymore.

"May I accompany you to Dana's wedding?" he asked sweetly.

"You're the only man I want to do that," she said and curtsied before his adoring eyes. "But, first, be with me in the receiving line. No one knows you yet."

The wedding guests and curious bystanders stared in disbelief as Leah crossed the street, her arm locked in Miguel's as they joined the wedding party and her family, now his family too. She always shocked those around her with the unexpected. Leah quickly introduced him to everyone, including the baffled Rocío, as her former seatmate and the man she'd love forever. He'd also dance the first dance with her at Dana's wedding.